DEMONS
ARE A GIRL'S
BEST FRIEND
THE REALM SERIES

A E   J O N E S

AE Jones: Demons Are a Girl's Best Friend

Copyright © 2018 by Amy E Jones

Publisher: Gabby Reads Publishing LLC

Cover Designer: theillustratedauthor.net

Editor: demonfordetails.com

PRINT

ISBN-13 978-1-941871-22-5

Author's Note

When I started writing the Realm books, I quickly realized that some of the scenes would need to crossover into the other books. Misha, Aleksei and Sergei's stories are interlocking in time—it's a close family, after all—so as you're reading the first three books, you'll probably notice some scenes you've read before...but from a very different perspective. Amazing what you can learn from a new point of view.

I originally planned on only writing a trilogy, but I couldn't get this family out of my mind. So two more books were born! Marrick first appears as Naya's loyal best friend in *Demons Are A Girl's Best Friend* and I wanted to tell this honorable demon's story.

And Boris...this over-the-top father and clan leader has a special place in my heart. How could I not give him a happy ever after?

Prepare for some fun with this outrageous but loving family!

Auntie Barb –
Aleksei, the hero in this story, is all about family so it makes sense that this book is dedicated to you. You have been the glue that keeps our extended family together. I hope you enjoy this version of an over-the-top demon brood who in no way resembles our family at all...

CHAPTER 1

Aleksei Chesnokov was a demon with a plan. If there was one thing he'd learned in his two hundred and fifty years, it was to have a plan and stick to it. As the future leader of the Shamat clan, he also knew his time would not be his own. Even though Boris, his father, was entrenched in his role of clan leader, and probably would be for the next several hundred years, it paid to be prepared.

He grabbed a towel hanging off the side of the treadmill and wiped his face, maintaining his stride even as he continued his morning ritual. Earbuds in, he listened to an audiobook. He was all about multi-tasking, so he listened while he ran. This particular book was about project planning.

Imagine a project plan is like a triangle. Point one involves setting objectives. Point two is establishing timelines. Point three includes determining cost. Each side of the triangle is necessary to ensure success.

Which made sense to Aleksei. He wished he could convince others of the importance of planning.

A plan provides balance.

Exactly. Aleksei strove for balance. However, over the course of the past three months, balance had become an elusive animal. It all started when he agreed to run the new Bureau of Demon Immigration. He had seen the job as a training ground for clan leader, a logical step in honing his skills. There were only so many business books he could listen to before he needed practical experience. So when he was asked to run the organization, he jumped at the chance.

Plus, how could he not help bring the demon clans from the realm to earth? The realm was a wasteland, a prison for demons who were being punished for a war their ancestors started a thousand years ago. To play a part in uniting the five realm clans back with the twelve earth clans was a weighty responsibility, and he had been proud to step up and assume the mantle.

Now? Now he wondered if he'd bitten off more than he could chew.

The alarm beeped on the treadmill he was pounding into the ground, and Aleksei pushed the cooldown button. Within seconds the speed adjusted, and Aleksei slowed his run to a fast-paced walk. He checked the clock on the wall. In a little less than two hours he would be meeting with the team to discuss the next group of demons who would emigrate from the realm.

Not an easy task, since these demons had no concept of earth and what living here meant. Food, clothes, language—hell, even their ability to change into human form—were all foreign to them. And to make matters even more complicated, the Bureau was now dealing with protestors, demons on earth who weren't happy about the realm immigration plans.

Once he finished his workout and took a shower, he would review his agenda items for the meeting. The machine slowed further, so Aleksei hit the stop button and stepped off.

Next he strode to the side of the room, entering a long, thin hallway with the bullseye at the far end, used for a special kind of target practice.

He could do this. Be the best damn director of the immigration. But he needed to convince Naya, the realm guard leader, that he was *not* the enemy. If she wouldn't disagree with him at every turn, things would run more smoothly. If only he could explain the concept of team-building to the stubborn female, but teamwork was not in her makeup.

Aleksei jerked back to the present and the droning in his ears, unsure how much of the book he'd missed by zoning out. Time to pay attention.

Step one in project planning: Imagine your objectives.

Aleksei stared at his palm. Sparks appeared and coalesced into a small ball of fire. Aleksei focused down the target range before releasing the fireball with a quick snap. The ball hit the center of the bullseye. He watched his hand again, ready to repeat the process as bits of fire swirled from his fingertips.

Practice makes perfect, and he couldn't afford to screw up—both for his sake, and the sake of his clan.

Naya ran along the realm forest edge, dodging between the trees to avoid being spotted by the demons ahead of her. She didn't understand why demons from two different clans were traveling together throughout the realm, speaking to everyone who would listen. Whatever they were spouting made the other demons anxious. And anxious was not a good state of being in the realm. Anxiety led to bloodshed.

Even though the earth demons had finally decided to allow the realm demons to come to earth, not everyone was happy with the change. Naya wanted the change...lived for it, actually. Before the "demon immigration," as the earthers called it, her days centered on keeping the realm demons from killing each other and from escaping their dimensional prison.

Now? Now her reality was changing, although much too slowly for her taste.

The demons Naya followed stopped, and she watched them from behind a large tree trunk. She tried to eavesdrop, but their conversation was muffled, even for her demon hearing. She could barge out there and ask them what they were doing, but her gut told her she would accomplish nothing other than scaring them away. And Naya always trusted her gut.

The demons split up, heading in opposite directions. Which one should she follow?

The crystal hanging around her neck heated beneath her armor plating. Kyle, her contact from earth, was reminding her it was time for the demon immigration meeting. She ground her teeth in frustration. She wouldn't be able to follow either target now.

She jogged through the forest to find a secluded spot to generate a portal to earth. She reached out telepathically to her second-in-charge, reverting to demon tongue.

Marrick.

Yes, Naya?

It is time for me to attend the earther meeting. You're in charge in my stead.

Be careful.

As always. Same to you.

And Naya, try not to disagree with the Shamat demon.

She chuckled as she continued jogging through the forest until she skirted a large tree into a clearing in the depth of the forest. This would work for her jump.

She attempted to relax in order to generate the portal, pushing away her frustration at losing the opportunity to follow one of the demons. How many *meetings* did they need to have?

Aleksei, the Shamat Marrick had referred to, was tasked with bringing the demons to earth, and to her mind he seemed overly concerned with making lists. He wore fancy clothes and uttered fancier words. There were no *agendas* in the realm, or *timelines*.

Naya didn't discuss next steps. She acted instead.

She was very young when she learned, quite violently, that actions mattered far more than words.

CHAPTER 2

Aleksei straightened his suit sleeve as he strolled into the Shamat demon meeting hall. It was time to get down to business.

First requirement for running an effective meeting: attendees...preferably on-time attendees.

He studied the group sitting around the large conference table. His father, Boris, sat one chair removed from the head of the table. As clan leader, Boris was used to sitting at the head, and Aleksei appreciated the concession his father made on his behalf.

Members of the Bureau of Supernatural Relations were also in attendance, including his brother Misha, and Misha's teammates Jean Luc and Kyle. The BSR members were, for all intents and purposes, supernatural detectives. They ensured that the various supernatural species got along, and didn't expose themselves to humans, who were currently oblivious to the presence of demons, vampires, and shifters in their world.

Kyle was the reason they were all here. If not for her impassioned plea to the Demon Council to allow realm demons to come to earth, his job and the Bureau of Demon Immigration would not exist.

Kevin Doyle, Aleksei's only employee, was there as well. Doyle was Kyle's suggestion. At first, Aleksei had hesitated. Doyle was a con demon, after all. But surprisingly, he turned out to be a great resource, with connections throughout the supernatural community.

As Aleksei took his seat, his babushka joined them. His grandmother had a tendency to invite herself to meetings, and since she was over a thousand years old, Aleksei was not going to argue with her.

He waited for her to get settled. He checked his watch. Everyone was on time—except Naya, of course.

Second requirement for running an effective meeting: an agenda. He set his tablet on the table and called up his agenda.

"Let's start the meeting, I have a lot of items to get through today."

Which was when Naya decided to make an appearance. First the far wall rippled like a waterfall. Then a pinprick of light formed in the middle and expanded outward until the circle grew into the size of a door. Naya stepped through, wearing the ever-present black one-piece jumpsuit and armor she wore while on duty.

Naya nodded at Kyle, but failed to acknowledge Aleksei.

"Apologies for being late."

"No problem," Kyle said. "Take a load off." She pointed to the empty seat next to Misha.

Except it *was* a problem, and Kyle wasn't the person to excuse her lateness.

Misha jumped up and pulled out Naya's seat.

Aleksei couldn't stifle the scoffing sound he made. Misha glared at him.

Aleksei raised his eyebrows in mock innocence. His brother was smitten with the guard leader, to the point where he couldn't form a coherent sentence around her. Aleksei could concede that she was a beautiful female, and he had only ever seen her demon form—tall, with long, dark hair, black eyes, and dark purple skin—but the moment she opened her mouth, any attraction he felt for her vanished.

"Let's continue, shall we?" he said.

And those were the last words he spoke before he lost control of the meeting.

Forty-five minutes later he watched everyone leave the room with their assignments. Assignments he hadn't given them, but assignments nonetheless.

He needed to rethink his effective meeting strategy. A bullhorn would be a definite asset during his next meeting—or, better yet, gags.

Only when the last person disappeared through the door and he was alone did he drop his forehead on the table with a thunk while a colorful Russian curse rolled off his tongue.

He was well aware that at the rate they were going it would take years to relocate thousands of demons from the realm. He didn't need the rest of the committee to remind him. He hoped they could increase the numbers significantly after the next group of twenty. But right now there were only so many resources available to handle the many moving parts of this project.

Which was when Doyle threw him under the proverbial bus in front of the team by announcing that they needed an office manager. Aleksei thunked his forehead on the table again. He wasn't ready to talk about new resources yet. He was still working on his plans for expanding the office.

But there was no stopping the team now. Between his father and grandmother, they would find an office manager for him. The words *slow down* were not in their vocabulary.

"I know you're hard-headed like me, son. But you shouldn't test it by thumping your forehead on the table."

Aleksei sighed before sitting up. He needed to pull himself together. If someone else had seen him like that, he would never have lived it down. His father wouldn't torture him—too much. At least he hoped he wouldn't.

Boris came to stand across from him at the table. "You're worried."

"Absolutely. We have so many to bring to earth, and now we have to worry about dissenters on earth *and* in the realm trying to stop us."

"Anything worthwhile is hard to accomplish. And I know you can bring this plan together."

He wanted to believe his father, but he didn't share his confidence.

And based on the glares Naya shot at him throughout the meeting, she wasn't sold on Aleksei's plans either. But then he didn't need her approval. Misha was the one falling all over himself to impress her.

Before Aleksei could respond to his father, Kyle returned with Naya, who was carrying a small duffle bag. Every time Naya attended their meetings, Kyle had something to give her before she returned to the realm. With Kyle, you never knew what she was up to.

Aleksei stood. "Before you return to the realm, I want to confirm that the portal guard is confident they can handle the uprisings."

Naya's eyes narrowed on him. "'Uprisings' is hardly the word I would use. As I said earlier, we've had some minor incidents. Nothing that can't be handled by the guard. I can ask you the same. Can *you* control your uprisings here?"

Touché. He probably deserved that, even though he hadn't meant to insult her with his question. She didn't trust him, or maybe the truth was she didn't trust his ability to get the job done. And even though he had decided he didn't need her approval, in truth her lack of trust bothered him. "We'll take care of things here."

Naya flung the duffel bag over her shoulder and reached for the staff resting against the wall.

Knowing she needed it for protection didn't sit well with Aleksei, either. Of course he would never tell her that. He thought...no, he knew...she would not take his concerns well. And even though he wasn't a betting male, he would lay odds that she could take care of herself.

The portal opened, and Naya said her goodbyes to Kyle before nodding stiffly at him and disappearing through the shimmering air.

Kyle rolled her eyes. "I don't know what it is with you two. Do I need to sit you in separate corners for a time-out?"

He ignored her comment. Kyle was just trying to rile him, which was her modus operandi whenever she came within ten feet of him. "What was in the duffel you gave Naya?"

"Wouldn't you like to know?"

"I question every day why Misha felt the need to make you an honorary member of this clan. I can only chalk it up to the fact that at the time he was suffering from blood loss."

Kyle raised an eyebrow. "I did save his life. And he didn't simply make me a member of the clan, he claimed me as his sister, which means I'm your sister as well."

"Yes. Although I'm sure I could try to revert the honorary status, claiming he was incapacitated and unable to make sensible decisions."

Boris appeared beside them and placed a hand on each of their shoulders. "Children, let's try to get along, or I will try this time-out scenario Kyle mentioned on the two of you."

Kyle laughed. "I'd like to see you try, Boris. I better get going."

Aleksei watched her leave. She never did tell him what was in the bag.

"What's the scowl for, son?" Boris asked.

"Nothing."

"I know the meeting didn't go exactly to plan. But, as I have learned over the years, things seldom go exactly to plan, especially when other people are involved."

"Is your advice coming from my clan leader or my father?"

Boris' eyes tightened for a moment, and Aleksei wondered if he was preparing to give him an earful. But a few seconds later his expression relaxed, and he smirked. "I would say a little bit of both. Just know I'm always here for you, my son." He clapped him on the back once before leaving.

Aleksei blew out a hard breath. He knew his father meant well, but his advice made Aleksei wonder if Boris really didn't have confidence in him. And, if true, did it mean his father would hesitate to turn the clan over to him when the time came?

It was more important than ever for Aleksei to prove himself to be the leader both his father and his clan could rely on.

CHAPTER 3

Naya strode through the portal with her staff raised. She never knew who she might run into the moment she landed back in the realm, so she braced herself accordingly. Luckily she encountered no resistance this time as she moved through the forest toward the portal to the in-between, the dimensional borderlands between earth and the realm that the guards called home when they were not on patrol.

She jogged along, working muscles that had tightened up during the meeting on earth. What was it about Aleksei that made her so defensive? He didn't fit in her world. He dressed in suits and was clean-shaven, without a dark hair out of place on his head. Perhaps it was because his cocky grin made her think he knew a secret about her, or perhaps it was his green eyes. No, his green eyes were irrelevant. She had spent her entire life standing up to demons who would rather fight than waste time with words. And maybe that's why he threw her off-kilter. Unlike him, words were not her strength.

She arrived at the group of huts that housed the portal guard. Naya called out greetings to several guards before stopping in front of her own hut, where Marrick stood waiting for her.

"How was your trip to earth?"

"Fine. They still plan to allow the next group to relocate to earth. Twenty this time."

"Good. That should help silence those who don't be-lieve the relocations will continue. I wish the number was greater."

Naya nodded. "As do they. They hope to start bringing greater numbers to earth soon."

Marrick glanced around to see if anyone was close by before responding. "Can we trust them to follow through on this?"

"I don't doubt their sincerity. I worry more about their ability to bring thousands of realm demons to earth. Have things been quiet while I've been gone?"

Time moved differently in the realm than on earth. She had spent an hour or so on earth, but more than half a day would have passed in the realm. She tried not to think too much about the time shift, or she would get lost in the seeming impossibility of it.

Marrick crossed his arms. "The patrols have not reported seeing any disturbances."

"I followed the two who have been traveling to the clans earlier today."

His eyes tightened on her. "And?"

"And I didn't discover much. They split up at the southern edge of the forest. I would have followed one of them if I hadn't been summoned to go to earth."

"You should not follow them alone, Naya."

She knew he spoke out of concern for her, but she bristled at his comment anyway. "The opportunity presented itself. When I saw them, I reacted. You would have done the same." Except she hadn't learned anything.

"We'll travel the forest while on patrol tomorrow. Perhaps we will find something." Marrick responded.

Marrick wished her good night, and Naya entered her cozy little home, propping her staff next to the door and setting the bag Kyle gave her on the floor. She would get to the bag's contents in a moment.

She stripped off her armor, one piece at a time. The only time she was without it was in her home. Immediately she felt lighter and freer. Going to the fireplace next to her two-person table, she knelt down next to it, and picked up the rock she used to start her fire. She struck it against a crystal rock, sending sparks on the wood, then blew on the kindling until a thin trail of smoke wafted up toward her. She blew again, and a small flame started.

Next she got her stew pot, set it on the hook over flames that were just starting to lick the wood, then spent several minutes cutting up root vegetables and placing them in the pot with some water and spices. It would take awhile for the stew to cook, but she wasn't hungry right now anyway.

She was more interested in discovering what Kyle gave her, and she had been patient enough. It was time to open her gift.

Lifting the bag up on her small table, she pulled open the zipper. A strange name for the odd-looking fastener, but it was what Kyle called it when Naya first asked her how to open the bags she sent her. In the realm they used ties and rudimentary buttons on their clothing.

She caught her breath as she pulled out the books and set them on the table, glancing over at the corner where dozens upon dozens of books were piled. Before she became the patrol leader, when the previous leader traveled to earth to report to the Demon Council, he would bring back books for her. Wordsworth, Tolstoy, Thoreau...the authors were numerous, and the stories and poems magical.

Now Kyle was supplying her with stories. Naya ran her hands over the covers. She was quickly learning about the types of books Kyle sent her. They were very different from the ones she read in the past. The mysteries fascinated her.

She loved to follow the clues, as Kyle called them, and determine who the killer was. Although the reasons why these people killed were confusing to Naya. In the realm, you killed in order to survive, not because you wanted money or fame. And Naya wasn't exactly sure what either money and fame were, or why they were so important they were worth dying for. She would have to ask Kyle about it later.

She ran her hand over a cover with a couple kissing. These books confused her as well. Being part of a guard which was predominantly male had lent itself to physical attraction at a certain level, but not to truly understanding what love was all about.

From what she remembered of her parents, they were somewhat happy together. Did it mean they loved each other? They had told her they loved her, but their deaths taught her that emotions could be your downfall. Opening your heart made you vulnerable, and the realm did not allow for vulnerability. It was best to treat emotions like a sickness to avoid.

She looked down at the cover again. She would tell Kyle she no longer wanted these types of books. She didn't want to read about couples and their happiness. It was not something Naya could ever hope for in her world.

Naya picked up another book and started flipping through the pages, but her attention kept going back to the book with the couple. She reached for the book and opened it slowly, turning the pages until she came to chapter one. She would read the first paragraph to see what the book was about.

It was a gift, after all. Kyle would expect to hear what she thought of the books the next time they spoke. Naya didn't want to appear ungrateful.

CHAPTER 4

Aleksei glowered across his office desk at Doyle, who didn't appear to be intimidated. It was a few days since the meeting, and this was the first time the two of them were able to sit down together.

"I wish you had talked to me first before announcing at the meeting that we need more help."

Doyle shrugged. "What was there to talk about? We do need more help."

Aleksei gritted his teeth. "I realize that, but there were other things I wanted to discuss during the meeting."

Doyle leaned forward. "Aleksei, it's okay to ask for help. For us to have any hope of bringing more demons here at a faster rate, it makes sense to have more people working at the Bureau. If it makes you feel any better, it'll give you more people to boss around."

Aleksei couldn't help but chuckle at his coworker's jab. "And if they listen to me as little as you do, I don't think it will make me feel any better."

Doyle laughed. "You love my honesty."

Before Aleksei could respond, there was a knock on the doorjamb. He looked up to find his brother Misha and Kyle framed in the doorway. Why were they here in the middle of the day?

"Is something wrong?" Aleksei asked.

"No," Misha said. "We want to run something by you."

Doyle got to his feet. "That's my cue to leave. I have to go out in the field and check some things anyway." He walked out of the office and shut the door.

Misha and Kyle crowded in front of Aleksei's desk.

"This seems ominous. Don't just stand there staring at me, spit it out."

Kyle smirked at him. "When have you ever known me to beat around the bush? We found someone for your office manager position."

He had naively thought he only needed to worry about his father and grandmother attempting to take over. "That didn't take long."

Misha nodded. "Her name is Callie Roberts. She has experience in both office management and also managing different sales accounts, and she would be a good fit for this project."

Aleksei picked up a pen and jotted the name down on the pad of paper he kept readily available on his desk. "Her name isn't familiar to me, which means she's not Shamat. What clan does she belong to?"

Misha and Kyle exchanged a cryptic look. This couldn't be good.

"Actually, Callie is human."

"And she is an expert on demons, how?"

Again with the hesitation and the looks. It was time to stop this train.

Aleksei shook his head. "No. I don't see how she would be a good fit here."

Misha glared at him. "Why will you not consider Callie for the office manager job?"

"She's human and knows nothing about us."

"Callie may be human, but she knows supernaturals exists. Her twin sons are half demon, and she wants to learn about us. She has the office background to help you as well.

You need someone who can dive in immediately, and we can train her about the demon clans along the way," Misha argued.

"I don't know." Aleksei needed time to think this through.

Kyle interrupted. "Aleksei, pull the stick out of your butt and listen for a minute. When we first created the demon immigration office, I took a big risk in suggesting you run it. To be honest, I didn't know if you could table your arrogance and play nice with others. But Misha agreed with me about giving you a chance. If he thinks Callie is a good fit, then let's give her a shot."

Aleksei narrowed his eyes at Kyle for a moment. She really could be a royal pain in the arse. "It's a good thing you're not our press secretary, Kyle. You are a bit too—"

"Honest?"

Aleksei shrugged. There was no use fighting them on this. Kyle was like a dog with a bone. "Very well, I will interview her."

"Great!" Kyle said. "She's in the outer office."

Forget canine analogies, Kyle was like a vampire in a blood bank. "You want me to interview her now?"

"Yes. Time is money, and we need to work faster to get more realm demons to earth."

Aleksei stood from behind his desk. "On that we agree."

Kyle hustled out of the office to bring the human he knew nothing about in for an interview. He tried to take a calming breath.

"Be nice to Callie, brother."

So much for remaining calm. "Or what?"

Misha didn't answer right away. "All I ask is that you give her a chance."

Aleksei stared at his brother before nodding. Did Misha honestly believe he would be so terrible to her? And if so, why would he expose her to him in the first place?

Kyle re-entered the office, escorting a small, blond woman with pretty green eyes. Eyes that widened as she looked up at him.

Misha spoke, "Callie Roberts, this is Aleksei Chesnokov. He runs the demon immigration office, and will be interviewing you today."

Aleksei nodded. "Callie. It's nice to meet you."

"Nice to meet you as well," she said quietly.

Aleksei glanced at Misha and then Kyle, who were hovering behind her. "Why don't you two give us some privacy so we can talk?"

Misha gave Callie an encouraging smile, and Kyle squeezed her arm before they both left and closed the door.

"They act as if they're leaving you with your executioner," Aleksei mumbled.

Callie's eyes widened again. "You are a little intimidating, sir."

Apparently not intimidating enough to Kyle and his brother. "Only to my enemies. Now, why don't you take a seat and tell me why I should hire you for this job."

She pulled a resume out of the folder in her hand and handed it to him.

After a few minutes of back and forth, Aleksei was impressed by Callie. She was smart, and had obviously managed offices in the past.

Misha poked his head into the room. "Sorry to interrupt, but Solomon is here and insists on speaking with you."

Aleksei stood. "Sorry, Callie. I have to deal with this. He's been incredibly vocal about his opposition to bringing realm demons here."

"Kyle's talking to him now," Misha said.

Aleksei rushed around his desk. "Damn. That's not good."

Misha frowned. "Is he dangerous?"

"No, I'm more worried about Kyle hurting *him*. Come make sure your teammate behaves herself."

Aleksei and Misha hurried out into the main office to find Kyle standing in front of Solomon, glaring at him.

"What can I do for you, Solomon?" Aleksei asked.

"I want a report on how things are going with the demons who have been brought to earth so far. We don't know how they'll react."

The office phone rang and Aleksei ignored it.

Kyle appeared ready to bite Solomon's head off, and relations with this clan leader were precarious enough as it was.

"As you know, only five demons have been relocated so far. They're in the process of getting acclimated, so there isn't much to report at this time. Of course we'll be providing more information at the next Council meeting."

"I think it is too soon to think about bringing a new group here."

"That's something we can discuss at the next meeting as well."

The phone rang again while Aleksei showed Solomon to the door, and Kyle left soon after him, once Aleksei made her swear she wouldn't hurt the Council leader in the parking lot.

For some reason, Misha tagged along when Aleksei returned to his office to finish his conversation with Callie. They paused in his office doorway to see Callie facing away from them, studying the calendars Aleksei tacked on the walls to track the projects. She was talking to someone on the speakerphone. Aleksei held up his hand for Misha to remain quiet.

"You mean the shipment on the twelfth?" she said.

"Yeah."

"That's three days away. How do you know you won't make it?"

"I'm short a man."

Aleksei cursed under his breath. The caller was from the trucking company they used. The program couldn't afford a late shipment. Aleksei took a step into the room, ready to jump in, but something made him hesitate.

Callie placed her finger on the calendar on the thirteenth and ran it slowly along the rest of the week before responding. "I understand what it's like to try to balance a business when you're short-handed, Manny, but we're on a deadline and need those materials. We've sent a lot of business your way recently, and would love to continue the relationship. Isn't there some way to make sure our shipment arrives on the twelfth?"

Silence. Aleksei opened his mouth, but Callie spoke first. "Manny?"

"Yeah, I'll figure it out."

"Thanks, Manny. I'll make sure to tell my boss how you stepped up for us on this."

Well, damn. The girl had spunk. Callie disconnected the phone, and Aleksei cleared his throat. She spun around, her face turning pink.

"You're hired," Aleksei announced.

"What?"

He was as surprised as she was by his proclamation. He didn't normally make decisions without weighing all the pros and cons, but he forged ahead. "You took care of things without being asked, and, from what I heard, you did it well."

She gaped at him. "I..."

"Is that a yes?" Aleksei asked.

"I..."

Aleksei glanced over at Misha. "Is she okay?"

"I'm fine," Callie finally replied. "I'll take the job, if the hours and salary work for me."

Yep. Spunk. "I like you, Callie Roberts. Let's negotiate."

A few minutes later, Aleksei watched Misha and Callie leave. He wasn't exactly sure what came over him earlier, but he felt in his gut that Callie was going to be a good fit. And, as much as he hated to agree with Doyle, they needed help.

If they ever hoped to speed up this process, they needed more people and more resources. By agreeing to run the Bureau, in Aleksei's mind he had sworn an oath. An oath he would fulfill, come hell or a stubborn female portal guard.

CHAPTER 5

Naya ground her teeth in frustration while she walked along the riverbed with Marrick on one side and her on the other.

They had been out on patrol several times and not encountered the demons who were causing trouble in the realm. In fact, the realm demons had been suspiciously quiet lately. As much as Naya hoped it was due to the demons finally accepting the relocation was going to happen, she wondered if it was really the calm before the storm. She had read the saying in one of the books Kyle gave her, and it fit.

Marrick held up his hand to get her attention, and she stopped. He pointed ahead. In the distance stood two demons—a Kelmar with orange skin, and a Majock with blue skin and black stripes. Since the demon clans rarely associated with each other, this was suspicious. Plus, Naya was almost certain they were the same two she had been following days ago.

Marrick and Naya set off toward them at a jog. It was time to start asking questions. As they got closer, the two demons turned and stared at them. Naya was surprised they didn't try to run. The Kelmar had a long scar along his face, and he smirked at her as a portal appeared. The Majock vanished into it, followed by the Kelmar, who gave them a small wave first.

"No!" Naya yelled as she ran toward the portal. She launched herself through the air...only to land on the hard ground when the portal disappeared.

She turned over and sat up, dusting the dirt off her armor.

Marrick glared down at her. "Damn it, Naya. What the hell were you doing?"

She didn't answer him, instead continuing to dust off her jumpsuit.

"Answer me. Why would you attempt to dive through a portal?"

"To follow them and find out what they're up to."

"You have no idea where they went or who was waiting on the other side. Are you trying to get yourself killed?"

"Of course not."

He reached down and held out his hand to her. She grabbed her staff off the ground, clasped his hand, and allowed him to help her to her feet.

"If one of the younger guard tried that, you would reprimand them."

He was right, but she was having a hard time admitting it. "True. But we know nothing of what lies they're spreading throughout the realm. And now that we know one of them is Abstatholm, we have a bigger concern."

The patrol's primary duty was to ensure the realm demons did not get to earth. While most of the demons had no way of traveling there, there were a select few known as Abstatholm who had the ability to create portals. And in the past those demons had been using their powers to travel to earth, taking other demons there and turning them into what Kyle called indentured servants.

It was why Kyle and her team had gotten involved months ago. When Kyle realized the demons who were imprisoned in the realm were descendants of the ones who were exiled a millennium ago, she petitioned for the realm demons to be allowed to come to earth.

"So we try to get the realm demons to speak to us and tell us what they've heard. It was impossible in the past, but now that relocation to earth is a possibility, maybe someone will actually be willing to talk."

Naya nodded. "It's worth a try."

Marrick folded his arms. "Anything is better than you flinging yourself through an unknown portal."

"Lead the way, Marrick. I'll let you speak to the demons. I'm not good with words."

"I think you are fine with words, but better with your staff."

Naya smiled. "Very true."

They hiked back along the riverbank toward the small valley that housed a group of Dragan demons. If they were lucky, maybe one of the Dragans would be willing to speak to them. Naya was still worried that a storm was coming, and she wasn't sure how they would fare when it finally arrived.

───◆○◆───

Aleksei pulled into the office parking lot, turned off his car, and scowled at his hands gripping the steering wheel. The last thing they needed right now was another setback. First Aleksei had received a call the other night informing him that the new demon halfway house they were working on had been vandalized. Doyle was forced to call in a cleanup crew, and Callie ordered new furniture to replace what had been destroyed. Now the new construction group he and Doyle had planned to meet with this morning cancelled at the last minute.

A light rap on his window startled Aleksei into looking up to find Doyle watching him with concern. He opened his door and climbed out.

"Can you get on the phone today and see if we can find another construction company to begin discussions with?"

"Of course," Doyle said.

Aleksei checked his watch. "Callie was going to run the conference call for us this morning, but it looks like we'll be on time after all."

They walked into the office building and down the hall toward the Bureau's office. Aleksei opened the main office door, and as he stepped into the room, Callie slammed into him and screamed.

Before he could find out what was wrong, she lifted her key ring up and sprayed his face with something. Searing pain stabbed him in the eyes as he was slammed back against the wall.

"Oh, no!" Callie exclaimed. "I'm so sorry."

Aleksei couldn't answer. Liquid fire ran across his face, and he groaned before smashing his hands over his eyes.

"Don't touch them. You'll make it worse," Callie said.

He ignored her.

"Doyle, push a chair over here and help him sit down."

Through his agony, Aleksei barely heard someone run toward the back of the office. Water turned on, and a few moments later steps ran back toward him.

A small hand grabbed his wrist. "Aleksei, take your hands away from your eyes. I have a wet towel, it will help with the pain."

He held out his hand, and she placed the towel in it. He laid it over his eyes and took a slow breath.

"What happened?" Aleksei grunted.

"Someone broke into the office and trashed it," Doyle said.

Aleksei pulled the towel away and attempted to open his eyes, but no dice. Everything was blurry. "Go see what the back offices look like."

Callie spoke from in front of him. "I walked in just a couple of minutes ago, and wasn't sure if they were still here, so I was leaving when I ran into you and defended myself."

He flinched as he rearranged the wet towel over his eyes. He had been felled by a small human female with a canister of pepper spray.

He would recover from the pain, but he wasn't sure if he would be able to recover from the humiliation.

Footfalls pounded down the hall, and Misha's frantic voice called out. "What happened? Are you okay?"

Callie replied, "I'm fine. I came into the office and found this mess and as I was leaving..."

Aleksei pulled the towel from his face and squinted at a blurry outline of his brother...and Kyle. Oh, no. She would never let him live this one down.

"I...ah...pepper-sprayed Aleksei. I carry a canister on my keychain." Callie reached for a new towel from a bowl of water and handed it to Aleksei. "I can't tell you how sorry I am."

Aleksei took the new towel and dabbed at his eyes. "It was an accident. I'm glad you defended yourself, even if it was against me."

Doyle joined them in the main room from the back offices. "For once I'm glad I'm short. I was behind Aleksei when Callie attacked him."

Callie put her hands on her hips. "I didn't attack him."

"You slammed your purse into him and then sprayed him," Doyle said with what sounded like humor. Aleksei couldn't tell if he was grinning or not.

"Neither of you were supposed to be here this morning. When I saw the damage, I thought you were the bad guys," she said again.

"Our appointment was postponed. How did you know something happened?" Aleksei asked Misha.

"The office panic button went off."

Doyle went over to the alarm panel by the door. "Yep, it's tripped. Probably happened when Aleksei fell back against it after Callie attacked him."

"Would you stop saying that!" Callie's voice rose.

"Callie, did you turn off the alarm when you came in this morning?" Misha asked.

"Yes. I typed in the code before I turned and saw the damage."

"So someone broke in here without disturbing the alarm."

"Wouldn't they need to know the code?" Callie asked.

Jean Luc spoke. Aleksei wasn't sure when the vampire had joined them. "Or a demon was able to short-circuit it with their powers."

Misha nodded. "We'll have to pull the video footage to see if we captured anything. I'm worried that if they were able to turn off the alarm, they probably sabotaged the video, too, but we'll double check."

"How do the back offices look?" Aleksei asked Doyle.

"Similar to the safe house. The bad news is, the computers are toast."

Aleksei struggled to his feet, even though Callie tried to get him to sit still. "Losing the computers is going to put us behind on the next relocation."

"Damn it! We need to call an emergency Council meeting," Kyle said.

That was not the path Aleksei wanted to go down. He held up his hand. "Let's think about this before we go to the Demon Council."

"We need to let them know what's going on," Kyle argued.

"Excuse me—" Callie said.

"I don't think we need to alarm anyone yet," Aleksei responded.

"I disagree," Kyle said.

"Hey!" Callie hollered.

Everyone gaped at her.

"We didn't lose our stuff."

"What do you mean?" Aleksei asked.

"I mean that I set up a cloud backup system for our computers a few days ago and backed up our files. We lost a day's worth of work at the most."

Kyle did a little jig, or at least that's what it looked like through Aleksei's watery, still-burning eyes.

"Oh, sister, I knew it was a good idea hiring you. I told Aleksei you were perfect for the job."

Aleksei swept Callie up into a hug. They all owed her for saving them. "You're an asset to this organization, Callie."

"Put me down, Aleksei. You're hurt."

He set her down. "I'll be fine in a few minutes. Demons bounce back faster than humans when it comes to injuries."

"I don't care. Sit down."

He let her push him down into the chair. She pulled another towel out of the water, wrung it slightly, and gently wiped Aleksei's eyes with it.

"I'm going to check out the video feed to see if we can figure out who broke in," Misha said, sounding angry to Aleksei. And did he just stomp out of the room? Something was going on with his brother, but Aleksei didn't have the time to think about it now.

Even though Callie's foresight saved their work, Aleksei knew they needed help if they wanted to bring the next group to earth.

He was demon enough to swallow his pride. He fumbled for his cell.

"What are you doing?" Callie asked.

"Can you open my contacts and call Boris for me?"

She handed the phone to him, and he set it next to his ear.

"Hello, son."

"Father. I'm going to need your help."

"Name it."

Aleksei filled Boris in on what had happened, and was surprised when, instead of feeling uptight about admitting he couldn't do this on his own, a weight lifted off his shoulders. They would need both the clan's help and Misha's teammates from the Bureau of Supernatural Relations to stop these vandals and bring the realm demons to earth.

Aleksei would figure out the details as they went along. This wasn't just business any longer. He would take off his suit and don a warrior's armor if he had to. He thought of Naya in her portal guard uniform protecting earth her whole life. If she could do that, the least he could do was bring the realm demons back home.

CHAPTER 6

Aleksei ended his call and glanced around his temporary office. His father had been able to house the BDI offices in the Shamat clan compound's community center. They moved into the space this morning, and Callie was out in the front office organizing everything. Even Misha had shown up to help them move in, which surprised Aleksei.

A light tap on the door had him calling out. "Enter."

Callie opened the door and peeked in. "Your father is here to see you."

Why was he not surprised? Aleksei checked his watch. "That's a record for him. He actually waited an hour before he came over here."

"I heard that," Boris called from the outer office.

Aleksei shook his head and stood. "I apologize for not warning you he was coming."

"I heard that too."

Aleksei rolled his eyes. "Welcome to my life," he whispered.

Callie giggled.

Boris stood in the doorway. "Did you not ask me to come over here so we could discuss the next Council meeting?"

Aleksei did his best not to sigh. "I mentioned that we need to get together, yes. I didn't expect you to show up this morning."

"But I'm here now, yes? So let us talk."

"Do you need me to stay here and take notes?" Callie asked.

"Actually I think it's a great idea," Aleksei replied. Maybe if she was there it would rein Boris in. "Why don't we have our conversation at the conference table?"

Several minutes into the discussion, Aleksei realized there was no buffer when it came to his father. While he appreciated Boris's assistance in their time of need, it didn't mean his father could now take over.

If they didn't convince the Demon Council to work with them, all their hard work would be fruitless. They needed to show a united front.

"Father, I understand that you're trying to keep peace with the Council. But if we don't convince them to step up now, it's going to get even harder as more realm demons come to earth. The other clans might not listen to you or me, but they may listen to their own clan leaders. And don't forget, Kyle is the spokesperson for this project and will be at the Council meeting."

"Ah, yes. And your sister does not have a diplomatic bone in her body."

"Kyle is your sister?" Callie asked.

Aleksei grinned despite himself. "She's not related by blood. Misha proclaimed her our *sestra* after Kyle saved his life. Although if you listen to the way she talks to me, you would think we were related. She is exactly what I would imagine an annoying younger sister would be like."

Boris chuckled before turning to Callie. "And now Misha has requested that your sons be made honorary clan members."

"I hope that's okay?" Callie asked.

"Of course, of course. We are happy to help guide your sons in the use of their powers. Misha has told me how great they are."

Callie's twin sons were a handful, which was why Misha had adopted them into the clan, hoping to teach them what it meant to be demon—including not letting humans know about their powers. It was a lot to take in for two seven-year olds whose powers had manifested earlier than normal.

The door opened, and Kyle strolled in.

"Speak of the devil, and she shall appear," Aleksei said.

Boris stood and took Kyle into his arms. "It is good to see you, my daughter."

Kyle chuckled. "I don't know what I'm going to do with you, Boris." She winked at Callie. "Are you having a fun time with these two?"

"So far," she said.

Kyle sat down next to Callie at the conference table and read what was on Callie's computer screen. The woman had no shame.

"Just as I thought. Talking about the next Council meeting. I figured I'd better be here to referee while you argue about the best way to handle the situation."

Boris sat again. "We are not arguing, Kyle. We are discussing the options."

"Have they been having a discussion or an argument?" Kyle asked Callie.

Callie looked between the two males. "Ahhhh, I would say they've been having a passionate disagreement."

Kyle plopped her head in her hands. "Oh, no. You've spent an hour with Boris, and he's already turning you to the dark side."

Boris laughed. A deep, belly laugh. "You are right, Aleksei, Callie is impressive."

"Yes, she is, which is why I told Aleksei to hire her."

Aleksei was never going to hear the end of Kyle saying, "I told you so."

Kyle clasped her hands together. "Before we decide what we should say to the Council, I think we should meet with Naya. We should find out how things are going in the realm, since it's something the Council is sure to ask about."

Kyle pulled a necklace out from under her T-shirt and began rubbing her fingers over the crystal she used to communicate with Naya. "I'll contact her to find out when she can meet with us."

Callie stopped typing and blinked at her in confusion.

Kyle explained. "Naya is telepathic. She gave me this crystal from the realm. It acts kind of like a conductor of telepathic energy."

Callie gaped at her. "I don't even know what to say about that."

"Sorry to throw yet another thing at you. You have to be on overload at this point."

Aleksei steered them back to the conversation. "We'll meet with Naya, but she is not going to tell us what to do."

Kyle batted her eyelashes at him. "Whatever do you mean?"

"You know exactly what I mean. Whenever we meet with her, she disagrees with everything we suggest."

"Naya is not used to having to discuss her decisions. Living in the realm means making split-second decisions to keep herself and others alive."

"Which is all well and good, but she doesn't understand how things work here. She's also stubborn and egotistical." Much like the woman arguing with him, but he refrained himself from saying so.

"Hmm." Kyle tapped her fingers against her chin. "Sounds like somebody I already know."

Boris coughed into his hand. Was his father laughing at him?

On second thought, maybe he shouldn't have refrained himself. "See how soon Naya can meet with us, Kyle. We should know exactly what we're going to say to the Council before we meet with them, including what Naya will say."

Aleksei could concede that it made sense to discuss this with Naya first. The last thing they needed was for Naya to anger the Council with her blunt style on top of everything else that had gone wrong in the past few days.

CHAPTER 7

Naya pulled off her armor and hung it on the wooden hooks by the door of her hut. She and Marrick had spent several patrols talking to, or attempting to talk to, realm demons. Many ignored them altogether, although a few had actually spoken to them. When they asked what message the two demons were spreading while traveling through the clans, they received some disturbing responses.

The demons were telling the clans that earth was not the paradise they had been led to believe. That the demons who now lived there were being oppressed by the earth demons. The irony was not lost on Naya, since it actually was realm demons who had enslaved those who passed through the portal. Now the earthers were trying to make up for it. But how could they convince the realm demons of this?

The demons didn't trust the portal guards. And now they had an Abstatholm who could travel to earth telling them they were being lied to.

Naya walked over to her fireplace and laid fresh wood on the embers, hoping to restoke the fire. Her necklace heated right before she heard Kyle's voice in her head.

Naya, can you hear me?

I'm here, Kyle.

It freaks me out every time I can hear you in my head, Kyle said.

Naya had to smile, even though Kyle wouldn't be able to see it. *Do you have news?*

Yeah. Unfortunately, it's not good news. We've had a couple of incidents here on earth. One of the homes we were preparing for the next group of realm demons was broken into and vandalized. The bureau's offices were also broken into.

Was anyone hurt? Naya asked.

Everyone's fine.

Will the immigrations continue?

Hell, yes! It will take more than some passive-aggressive jerks to stop us.

I don't understand all the words you just used, but I get the intent, Naya said. *Thank you for fighting for the realm demons.*

I'm not the only one. Aleksei already has new offices set up, and if he had his way, I think he'd faceoff with every Council leader. But that's not going to work for us in this case. We need to meet with the Council and explain what's going on so we can get their help. Prior to the meeting, we'd like you to come and speak to the group about what's going on in the realm. We have to plan out exactly what we're going to say to the Council ahead of time.

Naya didn't understand all this posturing, but she had been dealing with a lot of things she didn't understand since she met Kyle. *Fine. Signal me when you want me to come to earth.*

Great. So have you started any of the new books I sent?

Yes. I'm sorry I didn't thank you for them sooner.

No problem. I'm just wondering what you think of the stories.

The mystery was good, although I had figured out who the killer was by chapter seven.

Kyle chuckled. *You always do.*

One of the books confused me. It had a male who was a warrior in a faraway place. And when he came home, he didn't know how to act with his family and friends anymore. He still cared for his female, yet he told her he didn't want to be with her.

Yeah, that was a good book. He was damaged from his time in the army, and didn't want to burden his family and friends.

But isn't that what family and friends are for? Naya asked, although she wasn't an expert about either.

Yes, and people are too stubborn to realize it sometimes. But his girlfriend wouldn't give up on him and they got their happy ending.

It seems like these books always have a happy ending. If that's the case, then what is the point of reading them?

Because a romance book isn't so much about the ending. It's about how they find their way to each other. It's about them letting go of their fears to offer their heart to someone else. Which is a scary proposition.

Naya would face down a dozen realm demons before giving someone her heart. She couldn't even imagine letting anyone close enough to risk it. Instead she kept her heart armor-plated like the guard uniform she wore every day for her own protection.

Naya patrolled along an empty field and spotted a Lagfel demon on the other side of the open space. Instead of veering away from her like most realm demons would do, he hurried toward her. Maybe this demon was willing to tell her about the realm demons causing trouble. It wasn't a secret anymore that she and Marrick had been talking to whoever would listen. She stopped and waited for the male to approach.

He stopped a few feet from her and looked her up and down. "You're the one who has been asking questions. Why? The portal guard doesn't care what happens to us."

"I do care about you, and the rest of the realm demons. I want you to be able to go to earth if you want to."

"Lies. You want us to be made into slaves, to walk through the portal into a world worse than what we have here."

He dropped into a fighter's crouch and pulled a sword from the sheath on his back. Naya gripped her staff firmly in both hands and prepared for battle. He lunged forward, and she blocked him. He spun around, his blade hitting the bottom edge of her side armor before slipping down and slicing along her rib cage.

She hissed at the contact and backed up. Raising her staff, she swung it sideways and caught his jaw. He dropped to his knees, and she slammed the staff against his arms, knocking away the sword. Shouts came from the distance as other realm demons ran toward them. When he tried to stand, she cracked her staff against his leg, and he crumpled again to the ground.

Naya took off running toward the forest to camouflage herself among the trees. She ran for quite a distance before stopping to catch her breath, and when she pressed her hand against her side, blood coated her palm.

She couldn't stop to take care of the damage now. She ran farther into the trees until she was sure no one was following her. Only then did she create a portal to earth. She took a breath and pushed it out slowly before walking through the gate.

Aleksei settled at the conference table with Doyle and his father as the BSR contingent—Misha, Jean Luc, Kyle, along with their other teammates, vampire Talia, and Jason—walked into the room. Greetings were exchanged and Aleksei checked his watch.

Naya was late. Again.

Aleksei called the meeting to order. "We're here to have a preliminary discussion about what we'll report to the Council. What have you found out so far about the vandalism?"

Jean Luc leaned forward. "We have very little to go on. We interviewed the neighbors around the halfway house, and no one reported seeing the vandals. We have installed cameras at the house now, but there has been no activity since then."

"And the offices?" Aleksei asked, hoping they had some sort of lead.

Misha opened the folder in front of him and handed out papers. "The images from the security camera were wiped, except one blurry frame. I ran a number of programs to see if we could clean up the resolution. After a couple days, we've come up with this."

Aleksei studied the picture. The male was large, with black hair and a goatee, but it was hard to make out any specific facial features due to the poor resolution.

"This is the best the software can do. Unfortunately, this image is not something I can run through the facial recognition program. The best we can hope for is that somebody will recognize him."

Kyle looked up from the picture. "He doesn't seem familiar to me. Does anybody else recognize him?"

Aleksei shook his head.

Boris set the picture down. "I will show it to Mother. She knows everyone. If anyone could recognize him, it would be Irina."

"What about you, Doyle?" Kyle asked. "You still have connections to the seedy underbelly of the supernatural world, don't you?"

Doyle's eyebrows shot up. "Seedy underbelly? You know I've been legit for a while now, Kyle. Ever since you offered me this job."

"I know. But that doesn't mean you don't still have connections on the street."

"I'll see what I can find out."

Kyle steepled her fingers. "Okay then, are we still on target for the next group to arrive?"

"Yes," Aleksei reassured them. "The halfway house vandalism set us back slightly, but it shouldn't stop us from meeting our original timeline."

Callie stood, and Aleksei stopped talking to see what was the matter.

"I'm sorry. I have to go grab the power cable for my laptop I'll be right back."

Callie hurried across the large space, but stumbled to a stop as a portal formed in the wall in front of her. She looked back over her shoulder with a shocked expression.

"It appears that Naya decided to join us," Aleksei drawled. Could she not make an effort to get there on time?

Naya strode through the portal and looked around the room. "Sorry I'm late. I had to deal with a disagreement."

"What sort of disagreement?" Aleksei asked, alarm bells sounding in his head.

"More demons are questioning the plan to come to earth."

"Why?" Kyle blurted.

"Much like the protesters you have here on earth, certain demons in the realm do not wish for things to change."

Boris frowned. "The Council will not like hearing this."

Aleksei tapped his fingers on the table. Couldn't they hear some good news for once? "The Council doesn't like to hear much of anything."

"Maybe so, son. But without their support, we'll be unable to bring others to earth."

Aleksei couldn't sit still anymore. He stood and walked over to Naya, who had joined them at the table but remained standing. "Can your guards control the protestors?"

"Yes, for now. We need to make absolutely sure the next group can come to earth. If we continue to show the realm that moving here is a reality, the protests should die down."

"And we need to be able to demonstrate to the Council that the realm demons aren't all out to destroy us." Aleksei gestured to the empty chair between them. "Take a seat and we can bring you up to speed on what's been happening."

"I'm fine standing."

"Must we always disagree?" Aleksei asked in exasperation.

Naya shook her head and then flinched.

Aleksei's eyes tightened on her. "What's wrong?" He looked her over and saw a damp spot on her black jumpsuit. "Wait—are you bleeding?"

Naya lifted her hand from her side, and green blood ran down her palm.

Damn it.

Kyle jumped to her feet. "You're hurt!"

Everyone else jumped to their feet as well and they all started talking at once. Aleksei gripped the back of an empty chair when what he wanted to do was grab Naya and carry her to the infirmary. Which would not go over well. "You need to go to the infirmary and have the doctor examine you," Aleksei instructed, his voice sounding tight even to his own ears.

Naya waved away his command before grimacing slightly again. "I'm fine. This can wait."

"You need to be looked at now," Misha argued.

Of course she would declare she was fine. He had never met such a stubborn female. "We know you can handle the pain, warrior woman. But you're dripping blood everywhere. Go get sewn up in the infirmary."

Naya scowled at him. "Your concern for my well-being is overwhelming."

Aleksei's eyebrows shot up at her sarcasm. She could give as good as she got. "You don't strike me as someone who wants to be coddled."

"What is coddled?"

"It means babied," he said, hoping she would bristle enough to go to the infirmary. And by the narrowed eyes she shot his way, she was bristling. "You don't want to be babied, do you?"

"No."

He stopped himself from sighing in relief. "For once we agree on something. Kyle, will you please escort Naya to the infirmary?"

"I'm going, too," Misha announced.

Of course he was.

Kyle and Naya left the room with Misha trailing behind them like a lovesick puppy. Everyone sat back down except Aleksei. He couldn't get his heart rate to slow down. She was bleeding, and yet had stood there as calm as could be. What type of life did she lead, that she considered bleeding silently *normal?*

"Is she going to be okay?" Callie asked.

"She'll be fine," Aleksei said, looking down at his hands...which had a death grip on the back of the chair. He slowly unclenched his fingers and started to pace. It was time to make some plans. "Naya will stay here for a few days while she recuperates. We've suggested she spend more time here, and she has always rejected the idea. But she needs to learn more about earth and how to turn into her human side sooner rather than later." Plus, right now he didn't like the idea of her going back to the realm. Whether or not he could stop her was another thing.

Doyle spoke. "We should probably assign a mentor to her like we have with the other realm demons who've come to earth."

Aleksei was sure his brother Misha would be happy to volunteer to be her mentor, but for some reason it didn't sit well with him. He came to a stop next to Callie's chair. "I think Callie can be her mentor for a couple of days."

Callie glanced up. "Me? But I'm not a demon."

Aleksei shrugged. "She already knows how to be a demon. Naya needs someone who can teach her about earth. Plus you can explain to her how the immigration process works on our side so she can communicate it to those in the realm who'll listen to her." The more he said, the more he warmed to the idea.

Callie looked down at the table and didn't say anything.

"Callie, you didn't answer me. Do you have time to work with Naya?"

"I'll make the time."

Excellent. Now all he needed was to get Naya to agree to this. Maybe if he wasn't the one to suggest it, she might not fight it. Whose head would she not bite off? He looked down at Callie again and smiled. No one would bite Callie's head off. She would be step number one, but he needed to pull out the big guns for step number two, and his babushka should work just fine.

CHAPTER 8

Naya sat on a narrow bed while a female cleaned the blood off her side. This was what they called the infirmary—a place where the earthers took care of people who were sick or injured. Naya wrinkled her nose. The smells were foreign to her and burned her eyes. The strongest smell came from the flat bowl the female set next to them.

"This is going to burn when I apply it."

Naya nodded. She wasn't concerned about a little pain. Most of the time she took care of her own injuries.

A few minutes later a male walked into the room wearing a white coat and a strange-looking necklace.

"I'm Doctor Calvin. With your permission, I'm going to check your injury."

She nodded again, wondering why he asked the question. Wasn't she here so he could take care of her?

He pulled off the necklace and put the ends in his ears, holding the metal disc on the other end up to her chest.

She held up her hand to stop him.

"Sorry. This is a stethoscope. It lets me listen to your heart and your lungs."

"Why would you need to listen to those when my injury is on my side?"

"We believe everything in our bodies is interrelated. May I listen?"

She lowered her hand, and he placed the cold disc on top of the paper shirt they had her put on when she stripped earlier. He listened for a few seconds and asked her to take some deep breaths.

He stood back. "Sounds good. Let's check your side now." He pulled on the funny-looking gloves the female was also wearing and lightly touched her side. "It's not too deep. I think I can stitch it up here."

"My armor absorbed most of the sword strike."

The doctor pulled a tray over to the bed. His eyes widened when she refused the numbing medicine he tried to give her. She didn't need it. He then spent several minutes sewing her wound shut.

While he discarded the gloves, he said, "You need to take it easy until this heals."

Naya shook her head. "Thank you, but I need to get back to the realm."

He frowned as she pulled the top of her jumpsuit back on, but he and the female left the room while Naya put on her armor.

A few minutes later Misha and Kyle joined her. "What are you doing?" Misha asked.

"Getting dressed."

"You won't need your armor here," he said.

"But I will need it in the realm, where I'll be returning shortly."

Before Misha could reply, there was a slight knock at the door.

The small human female from the meeting stood in the doorway. "Sorry to interrupt." She looked at Naya. "I'm glad you're okay."

"Is the meeting over already?" Kyle asked.

"They're wrapping things up now. Aleksei asked me to come talk to you guys about...well, Naya." She lifted her hand in a small wave at Naya. "I'm Callie, by the way. We didn't get a chance to meet earlier, what with you appearing through the shimmery wall and then bleeding and all."

"Hello, Callie. What has Aleksei proclaimed should be done with me?"

"Well, he thinks you should stay on earth for a couple days to recuperate. And while you're here, you can learn more about the immigration steps and how to turn into your human side."

Naya frowned. "For some reason Aleksei seems to be uncomfortable with me staying in my demon skin all the time."

"For once I think my brother's right," Misha said.

"And if I don't agree with you and your brother?" Naya asked.

Callie interrupted. "Yeah. About that. Aleksei says if you don't agree...and he wasn't holding his breath—his words, not mine—that I should tell you the portal is closed on the earth side until further notice. Whatever that means."

Naya growled. The male was impossible. "And what am I supposed to do here in the meantime?"

Callie answered. "Aleksei asked me to be your mentor for the next couple of days. I can tell you about earth, and you can help me put together transition plans for the next group of realm demons."

Naya blew out a hard breath. If they were going to convince the realm demons it was safe to come to earth, she *should* learn more about their new home. "Very well. I will contact my second-in-charge and let him know I'll be staying for a few days."

Naya stood and said her goodbyes to Misha and Kyle before Callie escorted her back in the direction they had come earlier.

When they entered the meeting room, Aleksei was there with the elder woman who had been at some of their previous meetings. He stood when she walked into the room.

His eyes narrowed slightly on her before asking, "Are you okay?"

"Of course."

"Good, good. Callie explained to you about staying here on earth?"

"Yes."

He motioned to the elder, who had also stood when they entered the room. "This is Irina. She has come to invite you to stay in her home tonight."

Naya bowed slightly. "Thank you."

Irina waved her hand. "You're welcome, and no bowing is necessary, my dear. I live in the house next to the center. Since you are still in demon form, we will use the covered walkway between the building and my house. My son insisted on building it, since he apparently is afraid I'll melt if I go out in the rain."

Naya gaped at her. "Is your rain poisonous here?"

Irina chuckled. "No, no. It's just a saying. He thinks I'm delicate since I'm older."

"If you've lived a long life, wouldn't it make you stronger?"

Irina beamed at her. "Exactly! I like you, Naya. We'll settle in at the house and have a pajama party tonight."

"Pajamas?"

"Sleepwear?" Irina said.

Naya shrugged.

"What type of clothing do you sleep in?"

"I don't sleep in anything."

Aleksei coughed next to her, and she glanced over to see him looking like he was mad or in some sort of pain. He ushered them toward the door. "It's time to go home."

"Callie will meet with you tomorrow morning at nine a.m."
He turned to the elder. "Will you make sure she is at the east
conference room by then?"

"Of course, dear."

"Would you like me to walk you home?"

Irina shook her head. "We're fine. I'm sure you have some
work to do."

"I do." He nodded to them both before he and the small
human took their leave.

Naya frowned at his retreating back. He seemed relieved
to be escaping. Which made her mad. She had done nothing
wrong. So why did he treat her like the enemy?

◆○◆

Holy Fates, he had to get away from her. Aleksei practically
ran back to his office, leaving Callie trailing behind him.
All he could think about was Naya sleeping naked. And the
image was not going to go away anytime soon, if ever. He
shut his office door and paced.

He could no longer deny his attraction to her. Even when
she argued with him, his blood pounded. When was the last
time someone really challenged him?

When he saw the blood on her side earlier, he wanted to
first make sure she was okay, and then go through the portal
and destroy the realm demon who dared touch her. He
needed to get a grip. He had no time for such distractions.

In all the business books he read, they referenced having
a five-year plan. Since Aleksei had centuries to live, he had
adapted it to a fifty-year plan. He was going to run the
immigration bureau for the next five to ten years, until they
were able to bring back all the demons who wanted to leave

the realm, and then he would start thinking about finding a wife and having children. He had too much to accomplish right now to let a relationship muck up his plans. And the word relationship was normally not part of his vocabulary. So what was his problem?

He must be working way too hard. When was the last time he had even gone out on a date? He knew he had a reputation for being a player, but in reality, since he didn't have time for a relationship, he dated sporadically, never seeing a female more than once or twice.

He didn't want to raise their expectations. And he wasn't being egotistical—although he was sure others, especially Kyle, would disagree with him—but rather, because he had learned that some of the females he dated were more interested in his future role as clan leader than in him. If that didn't deflate his ego, nothing would.

He sat down at his desk. It was time to get back to business. Something he could control...or at least hope to control...if they could stop the protests in both worlds.

As for Naya? There was no controlling her or his thoughts of her. And now he was back to picturing her naked in a bed that looked suspiciously like his. Damn it. He would have to run extra laps in the morning to get himself reined in.

He needed to follow his fifty-year plan, and one outspoken female was not going to interrupt his progress.

CHAPTER 9

Naya sat down on the large piece of furniture Irina called a couch. She had read the word in some of the books Kyle gave her, but hadn't truly understood what type of seating it was until now. She stared around the room in awe. Even though it had tables and chairs like Naya's home, the similarity ended there. There were so many items sitting on the different surfaces. And everything was soft, from the couch she was sitting on to the textured material covering the floor. There were no hard edges.

Irina bustled into the room and clasped her hands together. "I contacted Kyle. She should be here in a few minutes. She's coming back to spend the evening with us."

"Are you telepathic?" Naya asked.

"No. I called her on the phone. A phone is a device we use to talk to people who aren't nearby."

Naya nodded even though she didn't fully understand. But then there were a lot of things she didn't understand about earth. A bell sounded and Naya jumped.

"It's probably Kyle." Irina opened the front door, and Kyle came in, carrying several bags.

She held up the bag in her right hand. "I grabbed some dinner for us. Minestrone soup and bread sticks. And Tony tucked in some cannoli as well." She held up her left hand. "And I stopped and bought some pajamas, since Irina said you don't have anything to sleep in."

Apparently it was taboo to sleep naked here on earth. Kyle handed her the bag, and Irina directed her to a bedroom. Naya pulled off her one-piece black jumpsuit and tried on the pajamas. They were made out of the softest fabric she had ever touched.

Now she was wearing the proper attire, she followed the voices to a room with a large table. Kyle and Irina had placed dishes on the table. There were bowls filled with fragrant soup and a plate with long, thin pieces of bread.

"The pajamas fit," Kyle said. "I'm going to shop for some daytime clothes for you tomorrow."

"I don't need any clothes."

"Humor me. You're going to be here for a couple of days, and you're trying to learn how to acclimate to earth. Clothes are the first step. Now sit down and try some of the soup. It's vegetables with some noodles."

"Noodles?"

Kyle picked up a spoon and scooped something out of the bowl, holding it up for Naya to see. "Noodles. Try one."

Naya took the spoon and placed it in her mouth. The...noodle?...was soft as she bit down on it, and it didn't have much flavor, but the red broth was savory. Kyle gestured for her to take a seat, and Naya sat and took another bite of soup. It reminded Naya of some of the vegetables in the realm.

Kyle dunked some of the bread into her bowl. "As much as I don't like to agree with Aleksei, I think it's a good idea for you to spend some time on earth."

"I concur, both about spending time on earth and about not liking to agree with Aleksei. He is an exasperating male. He very much likes to be in charge and hear himself talk."

Irina chuckled. "That's my grandson, all right."

Naya gaped at her. "Aleksei is your relation?"

"Yes. Boris is my son. He and Anna had three sons. Mikhail—who you know as Misha—Aleksei, and Sergei."

"I apologize for speaking about Aleksei in that way."

"Nonsense. You're voicing your opinion. In this clan I encourage every member to speak their mind. Which in hindsight is probably why Aleksei is so outspoken. That, and the fact that he will take over leadership of this clan someday."

"I know I give Aleksei a hard time, but I think he'll make a great leader," Kyle said. "He really has stepped up to organize and implement the demon immigration plan."

Irina picked up her spoon again. "Finish eating while it's still warm."

They finished their food and moved back into the room with the soft furniture. Naya sat at one end of the couch and Kyle at the other. Irina settled into the chair across from them.

"Tell me about yourself, Naya. What do you like to do when you're not patrolling?" Irina asked.

"I have my books."

Kyle nodded. "She has hundreds of books. All the classics. And she learned a dozen languages just by reading them."

"Really? I'm impressed. Do you know Russian?"

"I can read it, but I have never had the opportunity to speak it."

Irina beamed again. "I can teach you." She started with a couple of easy phrases, and Naya repeated them.

After a few minutes, Kyle held up her hands. "Okay, you two. I only understand the curse words, so you need to table this for later."

Irina laughed. "Mikhail should have taught you something besides swear words."

"He tried to teach me other things, but only the swear words stuck." Kyle tapped her temple. "I've been giving Naya new books to read. I have a book I'm almost finished with that I'll give to you next. It's got a secret baby in it."

"What is a secret baby?" Naya asked.

"In some books the female will have a baby but won't tell the male. He might go away when she doesn't know she's pregnant, and then he comes back and finds out he's a father."

Naya glanced at Irina for help. "This makes no sense. A female only has one or two cycles a year, and both she and her mate would know when she was able to procreate."

"That is correct dear, for demons. Human females can get pregnant once a month, and they don't sense their cycles the way we do."

"So you guys don't have to use birth control?" Kyle asked.

"No," Irina answered.

"So not fair!" Kyle said. "I'm jealous."

"This planet is overwhelming," Naya blurted.

"Yep." Kyle nodded. "Which is what the realm demons face when they come here. The more you learn about earth, the better you can help explain things to those who are transitioning."

"I don't know if they would believe me."

"Then you keep telling them until they do," Kyle responded.

"And we'll help too, my dear," Irina said.

Naya sank further into the couch. It felt like it was swallowing her up, and in the realm this would have put her at a disadvantage. She needed to be ready to fight at any second. There was always the underlying sense of danger. On earth the people were relaxed in their surroundings, except Aleksei. He didn't strike her as a male who relaxed much.

He was driven, which she could respect. And he didn't back down easily, or much at all with her. That was a good characteristic for a leader, however it didn't mean he didn't frustrate her. She'd learned things were done differently here on earth. She would have to be open to listening. But Aleksei also needed to be willing to listen to her as well. He was not a warrior. Did not understand the need to use his fists. If she could get him to listen to her as well, they all would be better off.

Naya shuddered as she left the large room in the community center that Irina called a kitchen. According to Irina, she went to the kitchen every morning to greet the guards who worked overnight.

The guards protected the community, keeping the Shamat clan safe. In the mornings Irina made egg sandwiches, which they could grab, along with a cup of coffee, before they went home.

Today many of the males stayed in the kitchen and ate their food. Introductions were made, although Naya would have a hard time remembering their names. Every time a new male came into the room and sat down, Irina's grin widened. Naya didn't understand what was so humorous.

After Naya attempted to eat the eggs Irina made, she asked if she could explore the community center. She wandered along a hallway and paused when she heard a rhythmic pounding to her right. She moved slowly and quietly to an open doorway and peeked inside. The room was large, with all types of machines scattered throughout, and mirrors along the walls. This world had a lot of mirrors. In the realm, the only time she saw her reflection was when the stream next to her hut was calm.

She quickly found the source of the pounding. A male ran in place on one of the machines, the short-sleeved shirt he wore clinging to his muscular back. She watched him, fascinated. He ran with power, as if wanting to bring the machine to submission. After a few minutes, the machine slowed, and he stepped off it, wiping his face with a cloth. Naya held back a gasp when she finally caught sight of his profile.

Aleksei.

So this is what his suit concealed. A shame, in her opinion. Then she scolded herself sternly. She shouldn't be thinking about him in such a way. He was an irritant, not an enticement. He strode over to the side of the large room to a glassed-in wall.

Seconds later, he produced a fireball in the palm of his hand and threw it. The ball landed in the center of the circle on the far wall. And he followed it with another, and another after that.

Aleksei was a warrior in his own right. And the thought heated her body much the way Aleksei's fireball would heat his hand.

It was time for her to leave. But before she could back away from the door, Aleksei glanced over his shoulder directly at her.

◄O►

He should have known. Aleksei sensed someone watching him, the heat of the stare running along his neck and back. His heart rate had been slowing down from his run, but now it jump-started again at the sight of her.

She took a step into the room. "What is all of this?"

"It's exercise equipment to help make us stronger and in better health. Here in the compound it's also used to train the children how to use their powers."

"And you exercise here every day?"

"Yes. It helps me clear my mind and prepare for the day."

She nodded before looking away. He was at a loss as to what to say. They had never had a conversation that didn't involve the demon relocation. He could do this. He refused to be tongue-tied around her like his brother. "Did you have a good evening with Irina?"

"Yes. She is a wonderful female."

"She is," Aleksei said. "She takes care of everyone in the clan, whether you want her to or not."

"She made food for the guards this morning. I was surprised so many of them joined us for breakfast."

The guards didn't normally sit down and eat breakfast. What was going on?

"Who did you meet?" he asked.

Naya frowned and pursed her lips for a moment before rattling off the names of several males. The common denominator? They were all single. Aleksei bit back a growl. She had been here for less than a day and the vultures were already circling. Not to mention Misha following her around like a puppy dog.

She ambled over to a machine and ran her fingers along the weights. "I didn't know Irina is your grandmother."

"Yes. She is very opinionated, but big-hearted as well. Irina practically raised my younger brother Sergei after our mother died."

Naya turned away from the machine and gazed at him. "I'm sorry you lost your mother."

Aleksei cleared his throat. He always had trouble talking about his mother. "She was an amazing female. The clan adored her, and she helped my father lead. They were so in sync that they finished each other's sentences."

"Irina said you will be the next clan leader."

Aleksei nodded. "Even though Misha is the oldest, our law of succession is based on strength of powers."

"So you have been groomed to take over."

"Since childhood." He couldn't remember not feeling responsible for the clan. "It will be an honor to follow in my father's footsteps."

"You are lucky to have a family to rely on," Naya said.

"What of your family?" Aleksei asked, although he dreaded what she was going to tell him.

"Both of my parents are gone now. My mother was Shamat and my father Pavel. As you know, in the in-between, the guards are able to mate with other clan members and have offspring, unlike on earth or in the realm. My parents took comfort in each other. They were honorable warriors."

He closed his hand into a fist to stop himself from reaching out to her. "I'm sorry you lost your family."

Naya shrugged. "My fellow guards are my family now."

No inflection in her voice. A simple statement of fact, as if she was saying the sky was blue and the grass was green.

What had their ancestors done to each other to create the chaotic worlds they lived in today? Worlds that were each lacking. They needed to find a way to bring them together again. Aleksei had to ensure it happened both for the realm demons and the guards.

Naya deserved a better life. He would make sure she had one.

CHAPTER 10

Naya cocked her head to the side as she studied the small human female sitting across from her. How had Callie come to work for the Bureau—for Aleksei? According to Kyle, not many humans knew about the supernatural, which was one of the biggest challenges of the realm demon relocation. Irina had explained to her that she could not go outside until she learned to change into her human form. So how did Callie fit into the Shamat clan? Was she mated to Aleksei?

Her stomach soured, and she wasn't sure why. She had asked Aleksei about his family earlier, but she hadn't asked him if he was mated. She studied Callie closely. The female was pretty. Yellowish hair—blond—with intelligent green eyes.

"Good morning, Naya. Did you sleep well last night?"

She shrugged. "It's hard to sleep well in new surroundings."

Callie straightened in her chair. "I hope to explain about our surroundings so you become more comfortable in them. Before we get started, can I ask you a few things?"

Naya nodded.

"On your visits to earth, have you ever left this compound?"

"No. I've never left this building, actually, other than through the connected walkways. I've come for several

Council meetings and discussions regarding the immigration plans."

Callie looked thoughtful. "Can you tell me about your realm? Describe your life to me?"

"Why do you want to know about the realm?" Naya asked.

"Because if I know what your world is like, it will help me tell you what you need to know about earth."

Naya's first impression was accurate. Callie was intelligent. "Our world is not advanced like here. The realm does not allow us to use technology. We live much like earthers lived hundreds of years ago. We live in crude huts and cook over an open flame. We hunt and grow our food. The border patrol lives in what is called the in-between. Our job is to patrol the realm to maintain peace and stop the realm demons from coming to earth."

"How do you know what earth was like before?"

"Books. The previous leader of the patrol traveled back and forth to earth to report to the Demon Council, and he would bring back books for me. That is how I learned English and several other languages.

"According to Kyle, the books I have are what she calls classics. When I travel here now, she sends books back with me. They are very different from the ones I previously read."

Callie made a note. "If you don't have technology, how do you move between worlds?"

"Portal jumping can be done in two ways. A small number of guards have been given the ability to jump between dimensions. This was provided by the demons of earth centuries ago."

"And you are a guard because your family volunteered?"

"My grandparents agreed to protect earth from the realm demons."

"What is the second way a portal can be formed?" Callie asked.

"Certain demons have the power to jump between dimensions. They're called Abstatholm. They're rare, but they exist in the realm, and are able to travel to earth."

"Wow."

"Can I ask you something now?" Naya asked.

"Sure."

"How did you end up working for Aleksei and demon immigration?"

"You mean, how did a human come to work here?"

Naya nodded.

Callie took a breath before responding. "My twin sons are half demon."

"Your mate is Shamat?" Naya asked a little too quickly.

"I don't have a mate. The twins' father never told me he was demon, and he was killed before the twins were born. I didn't even know the boys were part demon until my son conjured a fireball."

"That must've been a shock."

Callie snickered. "I'll say. Now I can laugh about it, but then I was terrified. I didn't know what was going on. Luckily, a shifter woman friend contacted the Bureau of Supernatural Relations, and that's how I met Kyle, Jean-Luc, and Misha. Even though I don't know what clan the boys are from, the Shamat clan very generously adopted us as honorary members. I work for Aleksei, and we live in the compound so the boys can learn about their powers."

Callie reached for the chair next to her and placed a stack of long, thin books on the table. "And speaking of my sons. They let me borrow their books to help me teach you about our world. Maybe you won't need them if you've been reading."

Naya picked up a picture book about food and started to page through it. "No, this is perfect. Much of the time when I read I don't have a point of reference for what the author has written about. I read a story recently that spoke of a giraffe. I couldn't figure out what it was."

Callie reached for a book and set it in front of her. "We'll go over animals as well. Once we have gone through the books, we'll move on to Google."

"Is Google an elder?"

Callie chuckled. "Not in the way you're thinking, but it can answer almost any question you ask it. It will really blow your mind."

Naya's started at her words.

Callie held up her hands. "Blow your mind is just an expression. It means you might be overwhelmed by how much information you find."

"I've been overwhelmed since I went to Irina's house last night, and this morning when Irina asked me what I wanted to eat, I didn't know what anything was." She shuddered. "I won't be eating eggs again anytime soon. It bled yellow when I poked it with the eating utensil."

"No sunny-side up eggs for you. We'll see about scrambled next time." Callie flapped her hand, looking embarrassed. "Sorry, I know you have no idea what I just said."

Naya looked down at the pictures of food again. "We should probably get started. Thank you for helping me."

They paged through the books, with Callie answering Naya's questions. By the time they finished, Naya's head swam with too much information, and she fully understood what it meant to have your mind blown. There was so much to learn. But she told herself to be patient. Not something she was necessarily good at, but she could try. Since she and Aleksei managed to have a civil conversation this morning, anything was possible.

———————◀○▶———————

Aleksei sat at his desk staring at his computer screen. How long had he been staring at the same email? He still hadn't read through it entirely. The office was quiet since Doyle was out in the field and Callie was meeting with Naya right now. The conversation with Naya this morning had been surprising. Under her armor and poker face was a complex female. He had actually enjoyed spending time with her.

"What is the smile for, grandson?"

Aleksei glanced up to find Irina standing in the doorway. He stood. "Nothing, really. To what do I owe the pleasure of your visit, Babushka?"

"Can't I come simply to check out your new digs?"

"Of course."

She wandered around the office for a moment before sitting in the chair across from his desk. He took his seat again.

"I'm glad you suggested Naya stay with me while she's here."

"If I hadn't suggested it, you would have stepped in anyway."

Irina chuckled. "Quite true. She is delightful."

Aleksei's eyebrows rose before he could stop himself. "Delightful?"

"Oh, yes. She is so smart...and beautiful as well, don't you agree?"

He shrugged. His grandmother was up to something.

Irina continued. "Well, I know a number of males who would agree with me."

He scowled. "Who? Security?"

"So you've already heard? Yes, this morning was quite lively. I don't remember the last time I have had so many males sit down for breakfast. And even though I'm a good cook, I'm not egotistical enough to think it had to do with my cooking."

"It's not like she would be willing to stay here permanently."

Irina smirked at him. "No? So you have been thinking about this?"

"No! I mean—"

Irina interrupted him. "Well, I think it is very sweet of you to be concerned about your brother."

Brother? "I don't understand."

"Why, Mikhail, of course. That you're worried about his relationship with Naya. I plan to discuss it with him today. After what happened at breakfast this morning, it is imperative for him to start courting her before someone else swoops in."

Aleksei ground his teeth.

Irina stood. "I'll let you get back to work. I've got to track down your brother."

Aleksei watched his babushka leave and took a deep breath. It was obvious Misha had a crush on Naya. It was just as obvious he couldn't even manage to talk to her. Unless his grandmother was going to do the talking for Misha, there wasn't going to be a lot of *courting* going on anytime soon. His heartbeat slowed down at the thought. He frowned. Why was he worrying so much about whether Misha talked to her or not? Attraction was one thing, looking for a relationship was another.

He had a fifty-year plan, and he was sticking to it.

CHAPTER 11

Naya ran her hands over the clothing lying on the bed. Kyle had brought a number of items for her to try, and she was overwhelmed at the variety. Who needed so many things? In the realm she wore her jumpsuit. She had two, so she didn't have to run around naked after she washed one. Which would definitely not work here, since they wouldn't let her sleep naked, even when she was under a blanket.

She picked up a pair of pants made out of sturdy blue fabric and pulled them over her legs. They fit her more tightly than she was used to, but they weren't uncomfortable. Next she picked up the top Kyle had called a tank and told her to wear under the shirts until they could go shopping for a bra for her, whatever that was.

She was pulling the tank down to her waist when someone knocked on the door.

"Enter."

Kyle opened the door and smiled at her. "Those jeans look good on you. They actually fit nicely. I think you should try wearing this white peasant top with it." She held up the top and Naya pulled it over her head.

"Yep. Great combo."

"Thank you."

"You're welcome. I took Talia with me, and she picked most of these out. I'm not very good at picking out girl clothes."

"But you are a female, and you're wearing clothes."

"Yes, but I live in T-shirts, jeans, and work boots most of the time."

Naya looked Kyle up and down. "Your clothes are very practical."

"Thanks," Kyle said, sitting down on the bed. "Once you've learned to change to your human form, we'll go out and buy the rest of your clothes."

Naya fussed with the hem of her peasant top. "I would like to see earth, but I am having trouble turning into my human form."

"Unfortunately, it's not something Callie or I can help with." She snapped her fingers and sat up straighter. "I'll ask Misha to help you. I'm sure he'd be happy to explain how to transition to human."

"That would be good." Although a small part of her wondered if Aleksei could teach her.

"Misha's here right now, training Callie's boys in the use of their powers. I told Callie how you and I met when Dalton and I got pulled into the realm, and how you saved us. I also asked Callie if we could join them later so you can meet her sons. We're going to have ice cream, which is one of my favorite things in the world. I can't wait for you to try some."

"I'd like that."

"Good. Now let's see how the other outfits work." Kyle held up a pair of tan pants. "Try these on next."

Thirty minutes later, Naya and Kyle were on their way to the community kitchen to meet with Callie and her boys. Naya had decided to wear the jeans and white peasant top.

When they walked into the kitchen, Callie, Misha, and two identical male children were sitting around the table with bowls.

The boys stopped their chatter and turned to her. Callie made the introductions. "Naya, these are my sons Matty and Luke. Boys, this is Naya."

The boys stared at her with wide eyes—she probably appeared intimidating in her demon form—before Matty whispered, "Pretty."

Naya couldn't help but smile. "Thank you." She went a step closer, then faltered when she sensed their energy. She quickly smiled again, hoping Callie hadn't noticed.

From the frown on Callie's face, Naya wasn't successful.

Kyle looked back and forth between them, then turned to Misha. "Mish, why don't you show the boys the media room? They can eat their ice cream and watch a cartoon."

He frowned, then nodded reluctantly before ushering the boys out of the room, all three carrying their bowls of ice cream.

Callie waited until the boys were out of the room before she spoke. "Tell me what's wrong, Naya."

"Nothing's wrong."

Callie's eyes narrowed. "You're lying. Why did you react that way when you met my sons? If something is wrong with the boys, you need to tell me."

Naya spoke softly. "They are not ill."

"Then what?"

Naya hesitated. "I don't know if I'm the one to tell you this."

"Tell me what?"

"I sense realm demon in your sons."

Callie sucked in a hard breath. "I don't understand. Can...can you tell what type of demon the boys are?"

"As with Kyle, I am unable to tell what type of realm demon the boys are."

Callie's mouth dropped open as she turned to Kyle. "You're part realm demon?"

Kyle nodded.

"I don't understand. How can this be possible?"

Kyle grabbed Callie's hand. "Remember how I told you I was working a case and got pulled into the realm? During our investigation, we learned that certain realm demons have been traveling back and forth to earth for years now. They were running a demon trafficking business, bringing realm demons to earth and selling them as indentured servants."

"So the twin's father was one of the people involved in the trafficking?"

"Possibly," Kyle said. "It is very rare for female demons to be born in the realm. So some of the demons who were traveling back and forth to earth were trying to impregnate human females."

"For what purpose?"

"We don't know for sure. Normally the realm is toxic to humans, but when I traveled there, I didn't get sick. Maybe the idea is to have children who can be brought back to the realm and survive. Or maybe it was to prove that the realm demons can come to earth and continue their species. Which could explain why the boys are so powerful at such a young age."

Naya nodded. "Realm demons are extremely powerful. They have to be, in order to survive. In the realm, demons must develop powers early to protect themselves."

Callie closed her eyes.

"Callie," Kyle said, "everything is going to be okay."

"You don't know that for sure."

"I know I'm living proof that a half-human and half-realm demon can live on earth and blend in."

"And I will tell you about the different demon clans in the realm. It will help you understand your sons' demon sides better," Naya said, trying to reassure her.

Kyle gave Callie a one-armed hug. "Everyone has your back, Callie. You don't have to do this on your own."

Naya watched the human female. She was a good mother, protective of her sons. She was sorry to have upset her, but not being truthful would have been worse. At least now they could better understand the boys' demon sides and their powers.

A short time later, Kyle and Naya sat at the kitchen table by themselves. Misha had escorted Callie and her sons back to their home.

"I didn't mean to upset Callie."

"I know you didn't. I'll tell you what I told Callie. It will be all right. She loves her sons, and will do anything for those boys."

"As she should. It is the sign of a good mother."

Kyle set a bowl in front of Naya and handed her a spoon. "You have to try the ice cream. It's yummy, but it's also cold."

Naya pushed the spoon into the cream-colored ball and scooped up a small amount. She brought it to her mouth and took a tentative taste. Sweetness burst on her tongue. "It *is* good."

Kyle grinned. "Yep. Wait until you try the chocolate." She pointed to the brown ball in her bowl and Naya took a taste of it as well. This time the cold food was sweet, but it had a bolder flavor.

"I've never tasted anything like this before."

"I used to think chocolate was better than sex." Kyle grinned. "Although I don't think so anymore."

"How is Dalton doing?" Naya asked, wondering why she hadn't seen Kyle's mate recently. He worked for the human authorities, and helped hide the existence of supernaturals when he could.

"Good. I hope he'll be home soon. He's traveling for work right now." Kyle took a spoonful of ice cream before continuing. "Is there anyone special in your life?"

Naya shook her head.

"That's understandable, given how much stress the guard is under. I'm sure it's one of the things you won't miss when this is over."

Naya put her spoon down. "What do you mean?"

"Well, when all of the realm demons who want to come to earth are here, you won't have to be a guard anymore."

Naya really hadn't thought that far ahead yet. She'd spent her life living moment to moment. The realm was about daily survival.

What would she do when this was all over?

Could she honestly move to earth and find a mate? Here was something else she had never thought about. She had never felt anything for her fellow guards but friendship. Even Marrick, her second-in-charge, was more of a brother to her. Green eyes and a cocky grin flashed in her mind. She started at the image. Aleksei was the last person she should be thinking about as a potential mate. Weren't mates supposed to at least like each other?

But if she was honest with herself, she did like him. Which scared her more than facing down a gang of angry realm demons.

CHAPTER 12

Naya's brain felt too full. Callie had been teaching her more about earth, but today some of the things they discussed were very hard to grasp. Like money. Callie explained that everything on earth was bought and sold rather than hunted, grown or bartered. But Naya still didn't understand how a piece of paper or bit of metal was worth anything. She wasn't sure how to even ask the right questions about it, so she said yes when Callie asked if she understood.

Now Naya was waiting for Misha to arrive. He was going to teach her how to change into her human form and, if she was honest with herself, she was nervous. So nervous she had convinced Callie to stay for the meeting.

The door opened, and Misha strode in. "Hello, ladies. Am I interrupting your training session?"

Callie shook her head. "We were just finishing up for the day."

"I told Callie you're going to help me with my human side, and I invited her to stay. She's curious about the process, in the event the twins can eventually change as well."

"Not a problem." Misha looked at Callie. "The boys might never change."

"I know. But it doesn't hurt to be prepared. I don't want to be totally caught off guard if it does happen."

Misha pulled out a chair directly across from Naya and sat down at the table. "For the clans on earth, demons are

born in their human form and do not change until early ado-
lescence, when they're about twelve or thirteen years old.
It's almost treated like a rite of passage for some clans. My
father taught me how to change for the first time. To change
into your demon form, it's about understanding your human
body and allowing it to expand into something greater. In
your case, changing to human is going to be about pulling
inward."

That was the most Misha had ever spoken to her, but it
made no sense. "I don't understand," she said.

"Here." Misha held out his hands across the table. "Let me
try to help direct your energy."

Naya gripped Misha's hands a little too hard.

He squeezed her hands briefly, and she relaxed her grip.

"Sorry if I confused you," he said. "I think I was jumping
too far ahead. Let's start with your breath. Close your eyes
and inhale through your nose, holding the air in for the count
of three before exhaling."

Naya closed her eyes and started the slow breathing.

"Keep doing that, but as you inhale, imagine the air going
to every part of your body, expanding your lungs, your heart,
pushing itself down your spinal column and into your arms
and legs, all the way to your fingers and toes.

"The breath you're pulling into yourself is energy, and it's
expanding through your body, all the way out to your skin.
Now think about your skin. Let that energy spread across
your skin. Now pull the energy inward. Absorb the energy
on your skin into your body and hide it away."

Naya's skin tingled, and she concentrated harder. But after
a few moments the tingling went away. She opened her
eyes and blew out a frustrated breath when she saw her
still-purple arms.

Misha squeezed her hands. "You're doing fine. I didn't
expect you to be able to change immediately."

"What if you show me how you change to demon and back again?" Naya asked. "It might help me understand."

Misha hesitated at the suggestion. "I... Well..." Misha's reply stuttered to a stop. He opened his mouth, glanced Callie's way, closed his mouth again.

Callie pushed her chair back as if to stand.

"Where are you going?" Naya asked.

"I think Misha will be more comfortable if I leave."

Naya's gaze swung back to Misha. "Is that true?"

Misha let go of Naya's hands. "I'm not uncomfortable with you being here, Callie. But I don't want to upset or frighten you when I turn."

Callie sighed. "In the past year, I've learned that my twin sons are part demon. They conjure fireballs, move things with their minds, and can blow things up. A few days ago, we discovered that the twins aren't your normal earth demon. Instead their father originated from the demon realm. My current job revolves around helping realm demons relocate to earth, and I have been spending time with the amazing female across from you while she has been in her demon form. While I appreciate you being concerned, I don't think seeing your demon form is going to give me the vapors."

Naya chuckled to herself. Callie was a warrior in her own right.

Misha's eyes twinkled. "Thank you for clarifying. I stand corrected." He glanced down at his shirt. "When I turn into my demon form, I'm going to get bigger. I'm not telling you because I think you're going to be scared, Callie. But I am explaining why I need to take my shirt off, since it's already tight. Otherwise I'll tear it during the change."

Misha reached up and pulled his shirt off over his head. Naya had to admit he was a good-looking male, but he wasn't Aleks— No, she was not going there.

Misha reached for Naya's hands, and she gripped his again.

Misha's eyes turned black. A moment later, his hair darkened as his skin turned orange, starting on his head and rippling down over his neck, chest, and arms. Red markings appeared over the orange. Heat ran up her arms into her chest.

"Can you feel my energy, Naya?"

She nodded. "Yes. It surged through you a moment ago."

"Exactly. Now, as I change back to human, pay attention to my energy, and see if you can mimic it."

Misha shrank slightly as his skin and hair changed back to their human colors. The warmth pulled away from her, and she mimicked him as best she could. Naya began to change. Her purple skin turned brown. She had done it!

"Very good, Naya. How did it feel?" Misha asked.

She took a deep breath. "Good. Thank you."

"Would you like to try a couple more times until you get the hang of it?"

"I think it would make sense."

Callie stood. "Thank you for letting me stay, but now it's time to get back to work. I have a long list to complete before the next immigration." She left quickly, and Misha watched her leave with a small frown on his face.

"Is something wrong?" Naya asked.

"I don't think so. I hope she isn't worried about the boys turning."

"She is a very good mother."

Misha nodded. "Yes, she is. Now, let us try this again."

An hour later, Naya stood in front of a mirror in the exercise room and stared at her human form. Her hair had lightened from black to dark brown. Her skin was a lighter shade of brown. And her eyes were no longer all black. Instead they were white with brown circles in the middle.

If she leaned in closer to the mirror, she could see specks of gold surrounding the black pupils. She looked *different*. And now she had a human form, she could leave the building, and eventually the compound. Even after what Callie had told her so far, Naya couldn't imagine what was waiting for her outside the gates.

But she didn't want to stay inside. She longed to go outside, *do* something. But she didn't want to do it alone the first time. Maybe she could ask Callie to go with her? She went down the hall to the demon immigration office and opened the door.

Callie sat at her desk with Aleksei standing next to her. Aleksei gaped at her when she entered, his mouth slightly open, but then he closed his mouth into a thin line.

What was that reaction for? His scowl stung. "What have I done now?"

"Nothing. I'm glad to see you have embraced your human side."

"Misha is a good teacher. He invited me to watch him train with the boys tonight." She turned to Callie. "I want to make sure you're okay with that."

"Of course. You're more than welcome."

Aleksei cleared his throat. "We were just talking about the training. Since Matty is still having trouble with his fireballs, I think I might stop in as well to see if I can help."

Callie looked surprised. "How nice of you to offer, Aleksei. But I don't want to interrupt any plans you have for tonight."

"No problem."

Aleksei excused himself and left the office. Was he so disgusted by her human form that he had to get away from her?

Callie closed the office for the day, and they walked together out of the building and down the street. Naya jerked to a stop and looked around.

"Are you okay?" Callie asked.

"Everything is so different here. Other than going through the walkway to Irina's house, this is the first time I've actually been outside the community center."

Callie gasped. "How silly of me to not remember. I'll tell you about things as we go. Why don't you come to my house for dinner? The twins would love to show you their playset, and they can answer more questions about what you're seeing outside."

Naya agreed, and they started walking again, Callie explaining different things along the way. Grass, trees, flowers, streets, mailboxes, a small furry animal called a dog that tried to speak to them, but Naya didn't understand the language.

Naya jerked to a stop again when a large metal cart rolled past them with people on the inside. "Is that a car?"

Callie beamed at her. "Yes. It's different from the pictures I showed you, right?"

"Very."

"Am I overwhelming you?" Callie asked.

"No."

"How did the rest of the training go with Misha?" Callie asked.

"Good. I believe I can control the changes now, but Misha said I shouldn't leave the compound until I'm able to hold my human form for more than twenty-four hours."

"That makes sense. I'm glad Misha was able to help you."

"He is a good male."

Callie nodded and glanced away.

Naya studied Callie for a moment. "You like him."

Callie blushed. "What? No..."

Naya held up her hands. "I'm sorry if I have made you uncomfortable. I have a tendency to be too blunt. Living in the realm does not allow you to speak anything but the truth."

"I...do like him, but he doesn't see me in that way—"

"What way does he see you?"

"As a charity case."

"I don't understand this term."

"Sorry. It means he is helping me because I'm a single mom who lost her job, and he thinks I need help with my demon twins."

That didn't make sense. "I've seen you take care of your sons. You love them, and that's what matters. Demon boys are a handful, even for those of us who *are* demon. I would think any child would need to be raised with the help of a clan."

"I'm human. I can't do what you all do, and I'll die long before Misha does."

Naya considered the problem for a moment. "Here on earth, is your longevity guaranteed?"

"I don't understand."

"Do all humans live to be elders?"

"No. Illnesses and accidents can take people earlier."

"So even when humans fall in love and mate, there are no guarantees they will be together until they both die."

"True."

"It's the same for demons. In the realm, long life is far from guaranteed. And here on earth, the same can be said. According to Aleksei, his mother has passed. Which means Boris is alone now. Do you think he regrets the life he had with his mate and the three boys they created?"

"Of course not."

She stared at Callie, wondering if she should tell her what she thought, and then decided yes. "Maybe the issue isn't the way Misha sees you. Maybe it's how you see yourself."

She frowned. "What do you mean?"

"I mean, if you don't feel worthy to be in a relationship, then how do you expect others to see you that way?"

Callie opened her mouth and then closed it.

Naya shouldn't have been so honest. "I'm sorry—"

Callie cut off Naya's apology. "No. You're right. Blunt, but right." She stopped outside a building. "You're pretty observant for someone who's only been living on earth for a few days. I thought I was supposed to be teaching you."

Naya grinned and shrugged. "We'll learn from each other."

"Sounds like a plan."

Maybe Naya should take some of her own advice. There was someone out there for her as well. Until now, the world she lived in had always been a deterrent, or at least that's what she told herself.

Callie went inside what she called a day care center and came back out with Matty and Luke, who grinned up at her.

"You changed to human!" Luke said.

"Good job," Matty exclaimed.

Naya smiled at them. "Thank you. Your mother invited me to have dinner with you if that's okay?"

"Yes," they chorused.

Luke grabbed her hand. "We're having macaroni and cheese and hot dogs tonight."

Naya looked at Callie. "You eat dogs?" She pictured the hairy little animal who had greeted them earlier and shuddered.

"No. It's just what we call them. They're not made out of dogs. You can have the mac and cheese instead."

Naya nodded, wondering if she could make up an excuse to skip dinner with them, until Matty also grabbed her other hand.

"We can teach you things too," Matty said.

Callie nodded. "Good idea, Matty. I could use some help teaching Naya about earth."

The boys tugged her quickly along the sidewalk and started pointing things out. Naya glanced back over her shoulder at a chuckling Callie.

There would be no backing out now.

CHAPTER 13

Aleksei entered the training center to find Misha standing in the middle of the room on the blue mats.

Misha pretended to peer at him. "Is that you, Aleksei? I barely recognized you without a suit on."

Aleksei glanced down at his pants and shirt. "Very funny, brother."

"I'm training the boys in here tonight."

"I know. I'm here to help."

Misha gaped at him. "Really?"

"Yes. Callie said Matty is having trouble with his fireballs, and I remember what it was like learning with father. I thought I would help."

"That is very thoughtful of you," Misha said, before narrowing his eyes at him.

Aleksei tried not to squirm under his gaze. Of course he wanted Matty to learn, but the impetus for him being there just walked into the room. The boys were holding Naya's hands as they tugged her into the training room with Callie trailing behind them.

He sucked in a breath. Naya was still in her human form. Holy Fates. She was gorgeous as a demon, and breathtaking as a human. When he saw her earlier for the first time, and she gazed up at him with big, brown eyes, his brain shut down. He should have run in the opposite direction. Instead, he volunteered to help train Matty so he could be a buffer between Misha and Naya, now that his brother had found his voice around her. Not honorable, he knew, but then his brain had shut down.

The twins ran over to them and stared up at Aleksei with wide eyes. He met the boys once when Callie brought them to the office, but it had only been for a moment.

Misha squatted down. "Hello, boys. Are you ready to train?"

They nodded.

"Good. My brother Aleksei has agreed to help with the training today."

"You're brothers?" the twin to the left asked.

"Yes. Aleksei can throw fireballs. We thought you might want to work with him today, Matty."

The twin to the right grinned. "Yes."

"Excellent."

"Are you ready?"

The twin to the left—Luke—held his hand up as if he was in a classroom.

"Yes, Luke?"

"Can we go to the bathroom first?"

"Absolutely. You remember where it is?"

They nodded and ran toward the door.

"Where are they going?" Callie called out to Misha from across the room.

"Bathroom break," Misha replied.

Callie grimaced and rolled her eyes. "I told them to go the bathroom before we came here."

Aleksei couldn't hear what Naya said to Callie. But then Callie's scream tore across the room as a portal appeared in the mirrored wall. A demon charged into the room.

Naya dropped into a fighter's stance. "Run!" she yelled over her shoulder to Callie as she changed into her demon form, grabbed a barbell pole, and held it like a staff. Two more demons rushed through the portal into the room, each bigger than the last.

The blue Majock demon in the front attacked, and Naya swung her pole in an arc, slamming it into his arms.

Callie stumbled back, but her movement caught the attention of a large, orange Kelmar demon with a scar down his face. He ran toward her, but seconds before he reached her, she flew back and landed in Misha's arms.

Holy shit.

Aleksei let a fireball free, and it slammed into the chest of the gray Lagfel demon, who wielded a machete. He launched another fireball to distract the demon while Misha ordered Callie to go for help. Aleksei ran across the room and slammed into the orange demon, who had now turned his attention to Naya.

Naya held her own against the demon she fought, and Aleksei attacked the orange demon with his fists as the gray one advanced on him. A barbell flew through the air and hit the gray demon in the shoulder.

The demon staggered back a few steps, and another weight hit him in the arm. The demon howled, dropping his weapon. Aleksei punched the orange demon in the stomach, and he bent forward. More small hand weights flew past them and pummeled the gray demon. He backed up through the portal and disappeared.

Aleksei flipped the orange demon onto the ground, pinning him with his forearm against his throat.

The blue demon Naya was fighting couldn't deflect the blow she landed with the barbell pole, and he escaped through the portal while she swung the pole again.

"Why are you attacking us?" Aleksei demanded the orange demon. "We're trying to help you come to earth."

"Lies," the demon choked out.

Shouts from his clan joining the fray, led by his father, sounded behind them. The demon used the distraction to his advantage, punching Aleksei in the face and diving through the gate.

Aleksei blinked though the pain and focused on the portal. Instead of closing, flashes of light burst through.

"Get ready. More are coming!" Naya yelled.

"Everyone back away from the portal," Misha shouted.

Misha picked up a blue mat from the floor with his mind—his mind!—and shoved it up against the portal opening. He gritted his teeth while he deployed the telekinesis that Aleksei had no idea he possessed to move a large piece of exercise equipment in front of the mat. Two other clan members pushed another piece of equipment against the mat as well.

The mat bounced as if someone was kicking it from the other side, and light burst around the outer edges.

"I can't hold it by myself!" Misha yelled.

Aleksei, Naya, Boris, and two other clansmen ran over and pushed against the machinery and mats to help Misha.

"There's no one left here from their side. How can the portal remain open?" Aleksei asked Naya while they fought to hold the machinery in place.

Naya looked around the room, ran over, and grabbed the machete lying on the floor. She lifted her shirt and placed it next to her rib cage.

"What the hell are you doing?" Aleksei yelled, panic gripping his heart and squeezing.

"I need to destroy my portal device. It's the only thing they could be using to lock onto this place."

"You're going to kill yourself." Aleksei ran over and took the machete from her. "Tell me what to do."

"The device is located under my third rib. Cut between the third and fourth rib."

Aleksei hesitated, his stomach twisting at the idea of hurting her.

"Do it. I'll be fine."

"Hurry!" Misha yelled.

Aleksei cut along her ribs, and Naya didn't flinch. As blood flowed down her side, he dropped the machete and reached for her ribcage, but Naya held up a hand to block him. "If you try to extract it, I'll die. I have to be the one to touch it."

He jerked his hand back from her, and she flinched while she pulled a small silver cylinder out of her side.

Naya placed the device on the floor and picked up a hand weight, slamming it down onto the cylinder. Moments later the light bursts ceased, and the mat stopped moving.

Boris went into command mode, ordering sentries to be posted throughout the compound.

Aleksei yanked the sleeve off his shirt and attempted to press it against Naya's side. She pushed his hand away, and he handed her his sleeve.

"Use this."

She held it out to him. "You're hurt too."

She reached for his temple, and he grabbed her hand and held it. After a moment, she backed away from him.

A voice called from the doorway. "It looks like you didn't need me after all," Irina said.

Boris glowered. "Mother. You were supposed to be in the bunker. What are you doing here?"

"I might be a thousand and twelve years old, but I'm still one of the most powerful telekinetics in the clan." She looked pointedly at Misha. "Or at least I used to be."

Aleksei flinched at her statement. His brother had been lying to all of them for years about his powers. Why? But now was not the time to wonder about it.

"Are Callie and the boys okay?" Misha asked.

Boris nodded. "Yes. She and the boys are in the bunkers with the rest of the children. Naya to the infirmary. Now," Boris commanded. "Aleksei, you as well."

"I'm fine, Father. We need to regroup and discuss next steps."

"I agree. We can have that conversation in the infirmary while you are both being attended to."

"Yes Aleksei, we know you're a warrior, but you're making a mess and dripping blood all over the floor." Naya threw his words back at him with a straight face.

Before Aleksei could respond, Boris barked more orders while he herded them all toward the infirmary. Misha called Kyle on the way and told her what had happened. She said she'd alert the rest of the BSR team, and they would join them at the compound.

Aleksei watched Naya closely to see if she was doing okay. She had finally consented to using his sleeve to stem the flow of blood. She had been willing to sacrifice herself to save them all. How could he not be in awe of her?

They arrived at the infirmary to find Doctor Calvin was already waiting for them. Word traveled fast. When the doctor turned toward Aleksei, he held up his hand to stop him. "Take care of her first."

Naya narrowed her eyes at him for a second, looking like she wanted to argue, but then let herself be ushered into a room. A nurse took Aleksei into an exam room and had him sit on a table while she pulled a tray over next to him and started to clean his wound.

The door opened, and out of the corner of his eye, Aleksei saw Misha walk in.

Aleksei didn't say anything, couldn't bring himself to even look over at him. He hadn't had a chance to think through what happened just now. To wonder why his brother had hidden his powers from his family, his clan. And now that the truth was out, Aleksei's whole future was in question. The clan leader was supposed to be the most powerful child of Boris, and it was no longer Aleksei. Misha stood in silence as well until the nurse excused herself to see when the doctor would be joining them.

When she left the room, Aleksei looked up at Misha for the first time.

"Do you have something to say, brother?"

Misha opened his mouth, but then hesitated.

He might as well rip the Band-Aid off. "Why have you been hiding your powers?"

"Aleksei—"

"Were you going to spring it on us all one day. Announce 'The joke's on you, Aleksei, it's my clan now?'"

"That's not it—"

Aleksei held up his hand and stood. "Is it a pity thing, then? Poor Aleksei has always wanted to lead, so I'll hide the truth, even if he isn't the rightful leader."

"No!" Misha yelled before lowering his voice. "Of course not. May I speak now?"

Aleksei crossed his arms before nodding.

"Back when grandfather and even father took over the clan, it made sense that they needed to have strong powers to lead. Now? Now, I think powers are less important than the ability and the desire to lead. I am not a natural leader. I have known this since I was a child. Yet if I felt there wasn't anyone to take over the clan once father is gone, I would step up and lead anyway. But I have also known since you were a child that you *are* a natural-born leader. I didn't want to take the opportunity to lead this clan away from you. I want the clan to have the best person to lead them, and I truly believe you are the best person."

Aleksei had trouble sucking air into his lungs. "I appreciate your confidence in me. But you shouldn't have hidden the truth. Your powers are part of you, and regardless of your feelings, clan law states that the progeny with the strongest powers is the leader."

Misha stared at him hard. "Then it is time to change the law."

His brother had surprised him. "I think you underestimate your ability to lead, brother."

Before Misha could respond, the door opened, and Kyle and Sabrina Miller, the BSR doctor walked in.

"I can't leave you guys alone for a minute without you getting into trouble," Kyle said. "I called Sabrina in case the doctor needed backup."

"The clan doctor is with Naya now," Aleksei said.

"I'm surprised Joe isn't with you, little one. You two seemed connected at the hip since he came home last night," Misha teased.

Kyle blushed slightly. "He's out in the hall."

Sabrina took a close look at Aleksei's face. "That's a nice gash. Let me sew it up for you."

Kyle stopped next to Misha. "Make sure he doesn't end up with a scar, Sabrina. He thinks he's sexy now. If he has a scar on top of it, we won't be able to deal with him."

Aleksei couldn't help but smile. "You think I'm sexy?"

Kyle sighed. "No. I said *you* think you're sexy."

Aleksei opened his mouth again to respond, and Sabrina held up her hand. "Enough, you two. Aleksei, you're going to have to hold still while I do this, which means no talking. And I know that's not going to happen unless I kick Kyle out."

Kyle chuckled. "I was gonna go check on Naya anyway. The rest of the team is out in the hall talking to Boris. When you've finished stitching him up, we're going to discuss next moves." Her smile vanished. "Boris has already gotten several calls from clan leaders. They're demanding an emergency videoconference in two hours. They don't want to wait until the actual meeting tomorrow to discuss what's going on."

"It didn't take long for the news to get out," Misha said.

Kyle opened the door. "I think the compound being attacked the day before the meeting to discuss the future of the immigration plan is too big a coincidence."

"Agreed," Misha said. "Someone's deliberately sabotaging this project, and it's time to figure out who they are, and how to stop them."

Aleksei's mind went into hyperdrive. There was so much to plan and so little time to do it. But before he could even think next steps, he needed to know if Naya was okay. And that scared him. He did not have time for distractions, especially of the stubborn and beautiful variety.

CHAPTER 14

Naya rubbed her fingers over the bloodstain on her new white shirt. The shirt Kyle got for her. The doctor had left a few moments ago, after sewing up her side. He asked her if he should expect to see her again in a few days, and she shrugged and responded, "Maybe." She wouldn't apologize for her life or her duty.

She looked at the shirt again, at the red stains instead of green. Apparently, her body was adapting to earth far more readily than her mind. This planet held the possibility of a new life for all the realm demons, and to have them come to earth and attack the very people who were helping them was not going to go over well.

There was a slight knock on the door before it opened and Kyle strode inside. "You okay?"

"Yes. But I ruined the shirt."

"Yeah, it was awful of you to destroy the shirt by cutting yourself open to save us all."

Naya glared at Kyle. "Actually, Aleksei cut me. Is he okay? The doctor should be with him now." She was still awestruck at his response to the attack. He had fought alongside her as a true warrior would.

"He's fine. I brought Sabrina along, and she's taking care of him."

What had Kyle told her about Sabrina? Oh, yes. In Kyle's words, she was a gorgeous succubus demon who had her pick of males. A growl bubbled up in her chest, and she swallowed it down. It was time to change the subject.

"Is Misha okay as well?"

"Yep. He's in with Aleksei. I think Sabrina and I interrupted a brotherly heart-to-heart."

"I don't understand. What do you mean?"

"Misha's secret is out. The family now knows about his telekinesis."

"Why would he hide such strong powers? What..." The reason slammed into her. "His powers would make him the next clan leader." Aleksei must be devastated. His whole world, the plans he spent so much time on, ripped away from him. She barely stopped herself from going to check on Aleksei.

Kyle's eyes widened. "Yes. How did you know?"

"Aleksei told me. We were talking about the clan and how important it is for him to continue his father's legacy."

Kyle stared at her for a few moments before responding. "Misha doesn't want to be clan leader. He thinks Aleksei is the right demon for the job. They're going to have to sit down and figure it out, but right now they need to figure out what to say to the Council. The Council has called an emergency meeting for tonight to discuss the attack."

Naya wasn't surprised. She'd spent time with the Council leaders in the past, and several of them weren't very enthusiastic about the immigration plan. They might not have said it directly to her, but much could be read in a person's eyes.

"They're going to try to stop the immigration."

"We won't let it happen. I'm sure Aleksei's already plotting what to do next."

Naya nodded. Aleksei would fight for the realm, and she would fight alongside him, for as long as he needed her.

Naya tried to absorb everything going on around her. Aleksei, Boris, Doyle, and the BSR team were all in the conference room getting ready for the meeting. She made sure Aleksei was okay. He had a white square taped to his face, and he had changed out of his bloody shirt.

Kyle tried to explain what would happen during what she called a video conference while Misha set up some sort of machine that Kyle said was a computer at the end of the table. They would speak into the computer, and the Council leaders would speak into their computers, and they could hear each other while the Council leaders' faces would all appear on the large white square attached to the wall. It sounded like magic to her.

Once Misha stopped playing with the computer and sat down, Boris spoke. "I think it makes sense for me to lead the conversation once we have the other clan leaders online. Kyle should sit next to me as well."

Aleksei frowned, but before he could argue, Kyle jumped in. "I agree. Sorry, Aleksei, but I don't think we want them to see your battered face when we're trying to defuse the building hysteria. By tomorrow, when they're here for the Council meeting, your demon metabolism will speed up the healing and you'll look much better."

Naya watched Aleksei closely. Would he agree?

"Very well." He nodded. "Let's quickly go over what you two should say."

Kyle and Boris glanced at each other before turning back to Aleksei.

When the meeting started, faces appeared one by one on the wall, like Kyle said they would. Under each face their name and clan name were listed. While this was wonderous to Naya, the arguments and questions the leaders were spouting were full of suspicion and fear.

The Valtram Council leader in the upper right-hand corner, by the name of Peter Solomon, grew angrier as the meeting progressed. "I can't believe we are still considering allowing these realm demons to come to earth. They attacked your compound, yet you sit there defending them."

Boris shook his head. "I don't defend the ones who attacked us. I defend all the other demons in the realm who want nothing more than to come to earth for a better life. We cannot condemn thousands for what a random group of demons did."

"We don't know if it was random."

The arguing continued for another thirty minutes, until Solomon demanded the Council take the vote now to stop demon immigration. Naya watched Aleksei throughout, and his tense body and narrowed expression told her he was barely holding on to his temper. She knew the feeling well.

The Dalmot demon leader in the second row from the bottom by the name of Amelia Watkins spoke up. "We need more facts before we can make a decision."

"Exactly," Kyle said. "We need more time to find out what's going on."

"Twenty-four hours should be plenty of time," Josiah Akers, the Pavel leader, said.

While a few Council leaders, including Boris, rejected the twenty-four hour time frame, the majority agreed to vote on the issue at tomorrow's meeting.

Boris turned the computer off, and all the faces disappeared from the screen on the wall.

Everyone at the table started talking at once until Aleksei shouted to be quiet. "We don't have much time. We need to split up and figure out who is behind this. I agree with

Kyle that it is too coincidental that we were attacked the day before we were supposed to meet with the Council."

Misha leaned forward. "I agree as well. Naya, you didn't tell anybody about when we were meeting with the Council, did you?"

"No."

"Which means someone from earth had to tell them," Misha said.

"And it was as if they locked onto Naya's portal device to keep the rift open." Aleksei added.

"Has anyone seen something like that before?" Kyle asked.

Naya nodded. "Guards are able to lock onto each other's coordinates. It's a safety mechanism to help in times of trouble."

"Do you think one of the guards is a part of this?" Jean Luc asked.

"I trust the guards with my life. It would more likely be that the rebels have gotten ahold of one of the devices."

Aleksei's hands fisted on the top of the table. "You mean they killed a guard to get the device."

"Possibly. I will reach out to my second-in-command to see if anyone has been injured or killed."

"I say we hit the street and see what Sylvia has found out for us," Kyle said.

It made sense that the team had gotten Sylvia involved. Kyle introduced Naya to Sylvia months ago. She was a human woman who had been running her own demon immigration service to help those demons who had been caught up in the demon trafficking. She had been instrumental in letting the BSR know what was going on.

Aleksei loosened his fists. "Father and I will start reading Council law to see if there's a way for us to stop the vote if all else fails. Let's meet back here at ten a.m. tomorrow to discuss next steps."

———————◄◊►———————

It was the middle of the night, and things had finally settled down after the Council meeting. Naya had wanted to talk to Aleksei to see how he was doing, but when they disbanded, he left with his father, and she did not have a chance to speak to him.

Now she wandered around, nodding greetings to the security guards Boris had stationed throughout the compound. When she walked into the community center, she found herself at the training room where all the trouble began. And she wasn't alone.

Aleksei stood at the end of the long glass hallway. A fireball hovered above his hand, and he stared at it for a long moment before flinging it to hit the bullseye on the far wall. Seconds later he created another one with his left hand and let that one soar. From the number of black smudges on the wall, he had been here for a while.

She stepped into the room, and he spun to face her, a fireball forming in his hand. "What are you doing up?"

"I couldn't sleep," Naya said.

"Me either." Aleksei turned and threw the ball.

She crossed the room toward him while he dusted his hands against his pants, stopping a couple of feet away.

"How is your side?" Aleksei asked.

"It will be fine."

His eyes tightened on her face. "I'm sorry I hurt you."

"You did the right thing. I would have caused more damage if I had tried to do it myself." She clasped her hands in front of her. "How are you doing?"

He raised his hand toward his temple and she said, "Not your injury, I mean about learning of Misha's powers."

He dropped his hand and didn't respond.

"Kyle explained that Misha has been hiding his powers. It must have been a shock to you. Have you spoken to your father?"

Aleksei shook his head. "Not about that. Our first priority is finding a way to continue the demon immigration. Whether I'm destined to lead the clan or not isn't important right now."

"And that's exactly why you'll make a great leader."

Aleksei's eyes flared at her words. She took a step closer and noticed a drop of red on the dressing taped against his temple.

"You're bleeding. Let me check your wound." She took another step, waiting for him to protest, but he didn't say a word.

Right in front of him now, she reached up and peeled away the tape. The stitches were fine. He hadn't pulled any out.

"Your stitches are fi—" Her thoughts evaporated when she saw the heat in his eyes, his gaze moving down to her lips.

"Do you like Misha?"

Why was he asking her this?

"What?"

"Misha likes you."

Naya shrugged. "I have spent enough time with your brother to know I'm not the one he likes. But he hasn't figured it out yet."

"I knew it! He has threatened me with bodily harm if I so much as looked at Cal—"

She placed her finger on his lips, stopping the flow of words. Then she leaned forward slightly, and his eyes shot up to meet hers. He reached out and wrapped his fingers softly around the back of her neck before guiding her face to his. Warmth shot through her as he rested his lips on hers. So softly.

Once.

Twice.

A moan erupted from her of its own volition, and his gentle kiss turned into something more. He pulled her against him, and a soft warmth exploded through her much like the fireballs he had flung against the wall.

He devoured her mouth as if he were starving. She had never felt this...this loss of control. It exhilarated her and paralyzed her at the same time. After a few more seconds, Aleksei pulled back slightly to gaze into her eyes.

"I shouldn't have done that, but I couldn't help myself," he whispered.

"Why shouldn't you have done it?"

"Because we're in the middle of a crisis right now. The timing isn't good."

She sighed. "Aleksei, not everything can be planned out. Sometimes it simply is. When is the last time you acted before thinking it through?"

"Just now."

"And was it terrible?" her heart thumped as she waited for his answer.

"It was the opposite of terrible."

"Then don't think too much about it. Allow yourself to enjoy it."

"I can do that."

"Good. Now we should try to get a couple of hours of sleep. Tomorrow will be a busy day."

He let her go, and she immediately missed his warmth. She would explore this with him at a more opportune time. Maybe they could teach each other. She could learn to plan a little, and he could live in the moment. It could happen.

But first they had a demon realm uprising to quell.

CHAPTER 15

Nothing. They had nothing. Aleksei concentrated on the speakerphone so hard his vision blurred. The BSR team had called in remotely for their morning meeting because they were still out searching for something...anything...to help with the Council meeting tonight. He studied the faces of those sitting at the table—Boris, Doyle, and Naya, each looking as bleak as he felt.

"So far Aleksei and I have been unable to find anything to stop the vote tonight," Boris said.

"What did you learn, Naya?" Aleksei asked.

"I spoke to my second-in-command. None of the guard are missing as far as we know. Several have been out on rounds for days now, but that's normal."

Kyle's voice chimed in. "We haven't been able to talk to Sylvia yet. Hopefully she found something that will help us. As soon as we hear anything, we'll report in."

Aleksei called an end to the meeting. Doyle excused himself, saying he planned to see if he could learn anything from some of his old contacts on the street.

When he was gone, Boris stood and addressed Aleksei. "I need to show you something."

"Did you find something in the clan rules we can use?" Aleksei asked.

"Not exactly." He looked at Naya. "You should join us, since this affects you too."

After Boris's cryptic statement, they followed him back to his office. Boris shut the door and locked it. What in the world did his father want to show them?

He walked to his bookcase. "Aleksei, I need your help moving this."

Aleksei helped him pull it away from the wall, then Boris reached behind his desk and pulled out a crowbar, got down on his knees, and pried up a few of the wooden slats from the floor. Underneath the wood sat a black metal box. Boris turned the combination lock until the top popped open.

"This box is made of lead to hide any energy signatures." He held up a small cloth bag and Naya flinched slightly.

"What is it?" Aleksei asked her.

"I sense realm."

Boris opened the top of the bag and turned it upside down over Aleksei's hand. A small silver cylinder fell into his palm.

"Holy shit, is this a—"

"Portal device," Naya said, finishing his sentence.

"Why do you have one of these? And why the hell didn't you say anything?"

Boris held up his hand. "Let me explain. When you first become Council leader, you take an oath. There are certain things we do not discuss outside Council doors. This is one of those things. It was passed from my father to me, and I in turn will pass it to you when you take over the clan.

"When the five clans were sent to the realm over a thousand years ago, and the guard was created, the Council wanted to establish some checks and balances. If for some reason we ever lost control of the portal guard and the realm demons started to come to earth, each Council leader was provided with a portal device to use as a defensive weapon."

"You could go to the realm and attack instead of waiting on them to come to earth," Naya said.

"Exactly. I've been thinking about what Naya said yester-day concerning the possibility of the realm demons locking onto her portal device. Once Naya confirmed it was unlikely that any of the portal guard had been compromised or killed to get their device, I knew it was time to bring this to light."

Aleksei closed his fist around the cylinder. "You think one of the Council leaders might be using their portal device."

"I pray to the Fates this is not the case, but someone on earth has to be feeding these realm demons information. How else would they have known to attack yesterday? And if they are sharing information, they could be using their portal device as well."

"And if you're correct, they could be planning to attack earth again."

"Yes," Boris agreed. "If the vote doesn't go in their favor tonight, they could stage an even bigger attack here or in another compound."

"And here I thought it couldn't get any worse," Aleksei said. "We need to tell Misha and the rest of his team. I'm surprised you didn't say anything months ago, when we were having trouble with the realm the first time."

"I had decided to tell Misha and Kyle, but before I did, they were able to stop the invasion."

Aleksei handed Boris the device. "I would lock it away so it can't be used as a homing device on the compound."

Boris nodded, put it back into the metal box, and replaced the slats and the bookcase.

Aleksei looked at Naya, and she nodded at him, as if to give him support, when he should be the one supporting her. If the Council voted against the immigration, the realm demons would never be free, and Naya would never be free as well.

Aleksei would not allow that to happen.

———◆◇◆———

They didn't have much time. The Council leaders would arrive shortly, and the BSR team had just arrived, bringing Sylvia with them. Beside her stood a demon Aleksei had never met before.

Naya went over with Aleksei to greet the team.

Misha made the introductions. "Naya, Aleksei, you remember Sylvia. This is Galim. He is from the realm." He wasn't one of the five demons they had already relocated, which meant he had arrived through demon trafficking.

Galim looked intently at Naya for a moment until she nodded at him. "You're safe. I won't take you back to the realm."

"Galim is hypersensitive to anything from the realm," Kyle explained. "He's come to determine whether any of the Council leaders have been hanging around with realm demons. Sylvia has been doing some digging, and she passed around a picture of the guy who trashed the bureau around the neighborhood. Apparently he's been telling demons for weeks that the Council would be calling a halt to the immigration."

Aleksei started to pace. "They've been planning this all along."

"Yep," Kyle said. "There has to be someone on the Council, or someone who works for a leader, involved. Otherwise they wouldn't know so much about what we're doing."

"Agreed." Aleksei turned to Galim. "Can you sense items from the realm as well?"

"Yes."

"Great." Aleksei didn't want to explain about the portal devices in front of Sylvia and Galim. "Thank you for helping us. Let's pick out the best spot for you to watch when the Council arrives."

Kyle looked like she wanted to ask some questions, but the first Council leader chose that moment to walk into the room.

Soon afterward the other Council leaders arrived with their entourages in tow. Boris greeted everyone in his normal exuberant style. Aleksei would never have his showmanship, but he had his mind set. Boris didn't do anything without a reason behind it.

Josiah Akers, the Pavel leader, entered with three aides, followed by the Haltrap leader with two huge males who were obviously bodyguards.

Aleksei greeted the leaders as well, while Naya headed toward the back of the room. Even though Aleksei mingled with the leaders, he also kept an eye on the activity throughout the room. Kyle and Misha were stationed to the side, with Jean Luc toward the front of the room.

Galim stood by the main entrance, concentrating on each demon as they entered the room. Kyle waved to Sylvia, and the small woman hustled over to join her.

Kyle asked her some questions Aleksei couldn't hear from where he stood, and from the frustrated look on Kyle's face, he assumed Galim hadn't sensed anything yet.

The last of the Council leaders arrived, and Boris started to usher them to their seats at the large conference table while their aides, bodyguards, and other staff took seats in the audience section of the room.

Galim walked over to Kyle and Misha. As they spoke, they looked over at the table, although Aleksei wasn't sure who they were looking at specifically. Then Galim gestured toward the Valtram leader, Peter Solomon, and Josiah Akers, the Pavel leader.

Aleksei wouldn't be surprised if both of them were involved.

"It's time to call the meeting to order," Boris announced.

Kyle took her seat at the table. As the spokesperson for the immigration project, she would not be left out of tonight's discussion.

Boris spoke a few words to summarize the situation before turning to the subject they were there to discuss. "Before we vote, the BSR team would like to report on the recent attack. Kyle."

Kyle nodded. "Our investigation has turned up some interesting information. For weeks now, rumors have been spread to the realm demon population that we plan to discontinue the immigration plan. And the rumors have been coming from demons on earth."

"For what purpose?" the Haltrap leader asked.

"To incite panic. To anger the realm demons into attacking us."

"Which they have done. Which proves they can't be trusted," Solomon replied.

"I tend to agree," Akers said.

Kyle leaned forward, and Aleksei wondered if she was going to jump over the table and strangle Akers. Misha must have been worried about the same thing, since he placed his hand on her arm.

"I have a question for all of you," Kyle said, looking around the table at the Council leaders. "Have any of you actually spent any time talking with those you want to condemn to the realm?"

"I have," Council Leader Watkins said. "Today I spoke to some of the demons who arrived in the first immigration. I wanted to understand what their world was like before coming to earth."

So Galim must have sensed realm on her earlier. "And what did you learn?" Aleksei asked.

"That they have been living in hell, and they want to have the chance at a life here on earth."

"Did they strike you as uncontrollable animals?" Kyle pressed.

"No."

"Anyone else?" Kyle asked. "Have you spoken to them, Council Leader Solomon?"

"No. I do not trust them. We have a delicate balance of power on earth. We don't need to add more volatility here."

"You seem to be the only volatile one here right now," Kyle said.

Solomon glanced over at his aide, who stood at the back of the room and Aleksei noticed the aide had a goatee like the blurry picture from the office break-in. The man shook his head slightly.

Misha sat up straighter and glanced at Jean Luc, who took a step closer from his spot along the wall. Aleksei knew something had passed between them.

Boris spoke up. "I think it is premature to cast our vote now. There is obviously something going on that we need to research further."

"I agree," Council Watkins said.

Solomon slammed his fists on the table. "No! It's time to stop all of this."

"What are you so scared of?" Kyle asked.

"These demons are monsters. My father told me how they destroyed our village. He was one of the few who survived. He moved with the survivors to a sister clan, and they were adopted in, but were never treated the way they were in their own clan. Do you know what it took for me to rise up to be the leader of my clan? I will not allow these animals to come back to earth to destroy us again."

"What have you done?" Boris demanded.

Solomon jerked to his feet. "What the rest of you should have done, but were too scared to do! Stop those monsters from coming to earth!"

"You convinced them to attack yesterday," Boris said as he got to his feet.

The other Council leaders leapt to their feet as well.

Solomon charged around the table and headed for the audience. He ran toward Irina, as if to grab her. Irina flicked her wrist, sending him crashing against the wall like a rag doll.

Before Aleksei could get to him, Misha pushed around the Council leaders and stood in front of Solomon. "You threaten my babushka?" he growled in a low voice.

The Council leader struggled to get to his feet. Misha jerked him up and slammed him against the wall.

A thud came from the back of the room, and Aleksei looked back to see Naya standing with her foot resting on Solomon's aide's chest.

Galim rushed over to them. "He is carrying something from the realm."

Misha searched Solomon's coat and pulled out a silver cylinder from his breast pocket. "This is a portal device like the guards use. You are planning another attack!"

Everyone started talking at once.

"Quiet!" Aleksei roared as he forced his way over to Solomon and Misha. "When are they attacking?"

Solomon glanced between them with wild eyes. "He should have already attacked. The bastard owes me, and he betrayed me."

Misha frowned. "Why do you say he owes you? What did you promise him?"

Solomon tightened his mouth and shook his head.

Misha pressed his forearm to his chest. "Tell me, or I'll send you to the realm myself!"

"He asked me about the human woman and her half-demon brats. I told him he could have them if he attacked."

Misha shoved Solomon into Aleksei's hands. "I have a bad feeling. We need to get—"

Galim called out. "A portal just opened up somewhere in the compound."

"Callie!" Misha roared as he ran toward the door, Jean Luc and Kyle following close behind. Boris hollered for two security guards to follow him, and he ran out of the room as well.

"You fool!" Aleksei yelled, slamming Solomon against the wall again. "If anything happens to Callie or her sons, my brother will make you suffer, and if he doesn't kill you, I will." He looked over his shoulder. "Guards! Detain everyone who came with Solomon, including his driver."

The guards jerked the aide up off the floor and cuffed two others from the audience. Aleksei issued orders for them to be housed in the detention center.

"Shouldn't we interrogate him?" Josiah Akers asked. Since Aleksei didn't trust the Pavel as far as he could throw him, he adopted a demeanor his father would use.

"We need to secure the compound first and ensure everyone is safe. Right now we have a portal breach. As soon as we know things are back to normal, we will provide the Council with the opportunity to question him." But not before Aleksei and the BSR team spent time with him.

The Council leaders murmured among themselves as Aleksei glanced to the back of the room. Naya was gone. He strode toward the back entrance, and she stepped inside, stopping him.

"Do we know what happened?" he asked, and the Council and audience went silent behind him.

"A Kelmar tried to grab the twins and take them back to the realm. But they're fine. Callie attacked him with something called a rolling pin, and he was already down by the time Misha and Jean Luc got to her. Kyle said the demon will be singing soprano now, whatever that means."

Aleksei smiled. "It means Callie defended her sons. Is she okay? Oh, and what about the boys?"

"The boys are fine, but Callie's shaken up. Misha is taking her to the infirmary. Boris told me to tell you to continue with the Council meeting. He and the security guards are ensuring we don't have any additional realm demons in the compound."

"Let's take our seats again," Aleksei announced.

"Should we really vote now?" the Haltrap leader asked.

"I think now is the perfect time to vote. At the very least we should vote to continue the immigration. If something changes down the line, we can always reconvene. Solomon was manipulating this Council, and it's time to take a stand and bring the realm demons home."

"I agree," Council Watkins said.

After a few more minutes of back and forth, the Council took a vote, Aleksei voting yes for his father, since no one would doubt what Boris's vote would be.

Half an hour later, Boris gave the all-clear and the Council dispersed. Aleksei was finally able to take a breath.

Naya came to stand next to him. "You did a good job with the Council. You are a natural leader."

Aleksei shrugged, when what he wanted to do was gather her in his arms. "I did what needed to be done. Let's go see how Callie is doing, and then I'm going to have a little chat with Solomon. Thought you might want to tag along."

"Absolutely. I'm sure Kyle will want to be there as well."

"I wouldn't keep her away. The immigration is safe."

"For now," Naya said.

"For now," he agreed.

CHAPTER 16

Naya stood in a room staring at the flat, square boxes called *monitors*. Unlike the previous meeting with the Council leaders, where they had only seen their faces on a giant white square, these small monitors showed an entire room.

On the first monitor, clan leader Solomon paced back and forth. The second monitor showed Solomon's aide in another room.

The third observed the Kelmar demon who attacked Callie. He was sitting on a bench quietly, and his calm demeanor made Naya nervous.

She reached out telepathically to Marrick. *We have captured the Kelmar responsible for the attacks. I need you to come to the compound with a pair of cuffs.*

Yes, Naya. I'll see you soon.

Naya broke the connection and opened her eyes. Aleksei stood a few feet away, staring at her.

"Are you okay?"

"Yes. I was talking to Marrick, my second-in-command. I have asked him to bring a special set of shackles. They will stop the Kelmar from trying to escape. Marrick will be creating a portal in the compound shortly. Can you alert Boris and your security that he's coming?"

"Of course. Give me one moment."

Aleksei spoke into the small device everyone carried. These phones would be useful in the realm for demons without telepathy.

"Okay. Done."

When Kyle, Jean Luc, and Talia arrived, Aleksei asked, "Is Misha not joining us?"

Kyle shook her head. "No. He's with Callie. Are we ready to question some demons?"

Naya explained about Marrick's impending arrival.

"What is so special about these shackles?" Kyle asked.

"It's the metal. It blocks the ability of the Abstatholm to open a portal. It will also serve as a shield so other Abstatholm cannot find him. I think it is similar to your lead here on earth."

"So how would you like to proceed?" Jean Luc asked.

"I think we can split up and question them," Aleksei said. "If I had to lay odds on who might tell us something, I would say it would be Solomon's aide. He looks like he's about to pass out."

Talia spoke up. "I'll talk to him."

"And I would like to spend some quality time with Solomon," Kyle said.

Naya watched the Kelmar sitting like a statue on the screen. "I will talk to the Kelmar."

"I'll go with you," Aleksei said.

The team split up and went to the different rooms. Before they could enter the Kelmar's cell, a compound security guard brought in Marrick and the cuffs.

"Aleksei, this is Marrick, my second-in-command. Marrick, this is Aleksei, the leader of the immigration plan."

The males looked each other over for a moment before finally holding out their hands for a shake.

"Let's get this over with," Naya said.

When Naya, Marrick, and Aleksei entered the room, the Kelmar narrowed his eyes on Marrick and the cuffs. The first show of emotion on his otherwise passive face. The Kelmar stood.

"Do not fight us," Naya said.

When Marrick walked up to him, the Kelmar jerked away. Naya took a step toward him as Marrick grabbed his arms and locked the cuffs on each wrist. When Marrick backed away, malice seemed to pour out of the Kelmar.

"Why did you attack the compound?" Naya asked.

Nothing.

"You obviously hate earthers. Why would you agree to work for them?" Naya pushed.

His nostrils flared. "I did not work *for* Solomon. I used him."

"For what purpose?"

"I want Markel's progeny."

Aleksei said, "That might have been your reason in the end, but you didn't know about the twins at first. Why did you agree to attack the compound the first time? And why have you been spreading lies in the realm about earth?"

The Kelmar shook his head. "We don't need your help, *earther*. You lock us away for a thousand years and now you decide you want to help us? Decree that we should come here and be beholden to you? You may have me, but there are others who will continue our plan."

And after his pronouncement, the Kelmar refused to answer any more questions from Naya, Aleksei, or Marrick. They finally left and joined Kyle, Jean Luc, and Talia in the monitor room. Naya introduced Marrick to the rest of the team.

"We saw most of your conversation," Kyle said. "He's not going to give us much."

Aleksei frowned. "We'll see how he is after he's been sitting in a cell for a while. How did the other interrogations go?"

Talia spoke first. "Solomon's aide was talkative. Solomon sent him to search out other realm demons who had been part of the slave trade to see if they would talk to him. He started spreading rumors through them that the immigration plan was going to stop and the realm demons already on earth would be sent back to the realm.

"He finally had a meeting with the Kelmar—whose name is Joran, since he refused to share it with you—and then introduced Joran to Solomon. Solomon and Joran agreed to help each other stop the immigration. And then he went on to describe what we already know about attacking the compound."

Aleksei nodded and turned to Kyle. "Did you discover anything else from Solomon?"

"That he's a wackadoodle."

"What?" Naya asked.

"He's mentally unstable," Kyle explained. "Paranoid. He basically carried on a conversation with himself while I was in the room, yelling about stopping the invasion like we were in a science fiction movie. I'm actually surprised he was able to plan anything."

"I think confronting him at the Council meeting broke him," Aleksei said. "We need to map out the next steps. It would be good if we could also find the Lagfel or Majock who attacked the compound."

Naya nodded. "I think they've gone back to the realm. Without Joran, their ability to come to earth has been limited. Marrick and I will start searching for them while we attempt to repair the damage done by the lies they've been spreading in the realm."

Kyle took Marrick under her wing for a few minutes to tell him a little bit about earth, with Talia and Jean Luc's help.

Naya walked outside and took a deep breath. A moment later she felt Aleksei standing behind her. She somehow knew it was him without turning around.

"This has been a wild few weeks," he said as he came up beside her. "Fighting rogue demons was not even remotely part of my plan."

She looked over at him. "Tell me about this plan of yours."

He ran his hand over his hair. "Are you sure you really want to hear this?"

"I wouldn't have asked if I didn't want to know."

"I have a plan for my future. In the business world, humans often call it their five-year plan. As a supernatural, I adapted the five-year plan into a fifty-year plan. I'll work as part of the bureau until we bring in as many realm demons as want to immigrate. If we can successfully bring larger groups to earth, I estimate it will take another five to seven years to finish the relocation.

"Then I will help with issues on earth as the demon clans learn to live together.

"Year twenty-five will be when I start looking for a mate. As clan leader..." He frowned.

"*If* I become clan leader, I'll need to marry and produce heirs, and I will continue to support the clan to the best of my ability until my father decides to retire and beyond regardless of my role."

What a foreign idea. She couldn't plan for the next week. Everything was in flux in the realm. And even if it wasn't the case, how did someone plan their life out for the next fifty years? She frowned. She knew the kiss they shared was an impulse. She had been the one to initiate it, after all, but obviously he wasn't looking for a serious relationship with her. Not when he had a fifty-year plan.

"Naya? Are you okay?"

She looked over at him. "I'm fine. I guess I wasn't expecting your plan to be so..."

"Detailed?"

"Yes."

He shrugged. "Preparation makes things flow smoothly."

"I'll keep it in mind the next time a demon attacks."

He frowned. "Do you think you'll still have problems in the realm?"

Naya nodded. "Yes. We still have the two others who attacked your compound to deal with."

"What can I do to help?"

"You can make sure the next group of realm demons can come to earth. That will help prove that the rumors are lies."

"I can do that. If I also tell you to be careful, will you not get mad at me?"

"Only if I'm allowed to do the same," Naya replied.

CHAPTER 17

Aleksei was bone tired. After dealing with finding out Solomon was behind the protests, then the fallout within the Council and the Valtram clan, and now the second group of realm demons arriving this afternoon, Aleksei had been working nonstop for over a week now. As they headed toward the warehouse to greet the realm demons, he settled back into the limo seat and went over the last minute to-do list on his phone.

One item stood out. Naya.

He had not heard from Naya, at least not directly. She no longer had her portal device, so she had traveled back to the realm with Marrick. Since then, Naya had been reaching out telepathically to Kyle to report in. So far the guard had not been able to find the other two demons who attacked the Shamat compound.

Aleksei wanted to hear her voice. To ask her if she was okay, even though he knew she would be aggravated with him if he kept asking her that. So instead he kept pestering Kyle. If he asked Kyle one more time if she had heard from Naya, he was certain she would tackle him to the ground.

The one good thing that happened this week was when Misha finally admitted he was in love with Callie. Of course the rest of the family had known long before he did. Callie had decided to move away, and if Babushka hadn't staged an intervention to help his clueless brother, he would have lost her.

And as much as Aleksei wanted his brother to be happy, he selfishly didn't want to lose his office manager, either. A little voice in his head also told him it didn't hurt that Misha wasn't pining over Naya anymore. But then he told the little voice to shut up.

Although it *was* a little sickening to watch his brother dote on Callie. They were definitely in the honeymoon stage, and Aleksei decided he needed to suck it up and get used to it. Knowing his brother, Misha would probably never move past the doting honeymoon stage.

"Earth to Aleksei!"

He looked up from his phone at Kyle sitting across from him in the limo.

"There you are. For a second there I thought I was going to have to go get Sabrina to check you. Are you okay?"

"Yes. I was making sure everything is ready for our arrivals."

"Callie and Doyle have everything under control. You ready to check out the warehouse?"

He nodded, and they got out and entered the warehouse where the twenty realm demons would be arriving soon. Inside were several stations ready to check in the new immigrants. Callie sat at one table arranging the paperwork, while Sabrina and the compound doctor would provide cursory exams to determine if any of the twenty would need immediate medical attention.

Doyle spoke to the mentors, who would be working one-on-one with the realm demons for the next several days to help them get over the shock of acclimating to their new world. Many of the mentors were realm demons who had been brought to earth through demon trafficking, but were now being helped by Sylvia. The five demons from the first group of immigrants were also in attendance. Aleksei hoped that by seeing their fellow realm demons, the new immigrants would be comforted.

Aleksei looked around the perimeter of the warehouse. Due to the recent events, they had also beefed up security. However, the guards were told to hang back as best they could so they wouldn't spook the new arrivals.

"Appears everything is under control," Aleksei said.

"Like you would let it be any other way, control freak," Kyle said with a grin.

"I didn't want to face your wrath," Aleksei countered.

"Or Naya's wrath."

He looked over at Kyle, and she held up a staying hand.

"Before you ask, she hasn't reported anything to me since the last time you asked me. You can ask her for a full report yourself."

"She's coming today?" he asked, way too quickly.

Kyle gazed at him for a drawn-out moment before saying, "Yep."

"Good. I want to discuss some new ideas with her."

Kyle's eyebrows rose. "I'm sure she'll love the input."

Aleksei made an exasperated noise. "Must you be so sarcastic?"

"I must. It's like blinking. I don't even know I'm doing it."

"Why don't you go distract Misha? He's hovering over Callie, and she needs to get ready."

"I'll try, but after that Kelmar attacked her, he isn't going to be farther than arm's reach away. Plus they're so cute together."

Aleksei rolled his eyes before Kyle crossed the room laughing. He took a deep breath as the portal formed on the far wall. "Places, everyone!"

Everything had to go to plan. He had several immediate tasks to complete, but his attention kept wandering back to the portal to watch for Naya.

He had a plan to run by her. He just needed to figure out the best way to convince her it made sense.

Two hours later, Aleksei actually smiled. The twenty realm demons had come through the portal, and were immediately matched to a mentor, who led them through the medical exam. They also picked out clothes to wear to their assigned halfway houses. Each halfway house was staffed with two full-time demons who would be available twenty-four seven. For the next week, the mentors would be spending time every day with the new arrivals, and the newbies would also be attending class to learn the basics.

Once they were done here, since they were still in demon form, they would be taken in windowless vans to the houses and would exit directly from the garage into the house.

The process was running smoothly so far, but the new realm demons had to start with baby steps before they could run. And, of course, they had to remain under wraps until they could take on and maintain their human forms.

He glanced around the warehouse until he locked onto Naya. Aleksei had been way too happy to see her emerge through the gate, until the large, purple Pavel demon arrived with her. Marrick. He hadn't left her side since they arrived, and Aleksei wanted to speak with her. Alone.

He headed toward her, and the male watched him closely.

"Naya. It's good to see you again. Marrick."

The large demon nodded.

"Naya, could I please speak to you for a moment, alone?" Aleksei asked.

Naya narrowed her eyes at him, as if she was about to refuse. Aleksei beckoned for her to walk with him over to a small room at the edge of the warehouse.

"Kyle said you haven't been able to track the two demons who attacked the compound."

"No," Naya said. "Even with the immigration today, there is still a great deal of mistrust in the realm. We are trying to find the others involved, but it's proving difficult."

"I don't blame them. I've been thinking about what Kyle said during the Council meeting. She asked the leaders if any of them had spent time talking with the realm demons so they could understand where they were coming from. And I realized her question goes both ways. The demons still living in the realm also have nothing but rumors and hearsay to go by. We need to change that."

"And how do you propose to achieve that?" Naya asked.

"We need to provide them with someone to talk to from earth. It makes sense to send a spokesperson to the realm."

"And who would that be?"

"Initially, I would go."

Naya's eyebrows rose. "You? Come to the realm?"

Aleksei's mouth curled up. "Your confidence is overwhelming. If I can discuss their concerns with some of the leaders in the clans, show my face so the realm demons are aware that we're taking this seriously, it might help stop the dissenters."

"Are you sure about this? Don't you need to be here to plan the next relocations?"

"Someone told me recently that it's a mistake to spend so much time planning. Callie and Doyle can handle the logistics while I'm gone. I think we have to build trust within the realm or they will continue to fight us."

Naya stared at him for a moment before speaking. "Your idea has merit. However, I would first like to confer with Marrick to get his thoughts on this."

"Of course." Aleksei worked hard to keep the snark out of his voice, when what he wanted to say was *What the hell does Marrick have to do with anything?*

Naya stood outside the building, filling her lungs with fresh air. She would soon be returning to a world that smelled dusty and stale. Until she had spent time on earth, she had not realized how depressing it was in the realm. Even the atmosphere there pushed you down, held you back, as if to say there was no hope.

She had been shocked at Aleksei's suggestion earlier. When she first met him, she couldn't imagine him being comfortable in the realm. But he was much more than his expensive suits. She knew he wasn't afraid to fight. Which was something he needed to be prepared to do if he came with her to the realm.

She had hoped Marrick would disagree with Aleksei's plan. Instead, he thought it might help alleviate the brewing trouble. She should be inside discussing this with Aleksei, but she couldn't bring herself to do it. If he was going to come to the realm, he would need to be willing to follow her rules, her direction.

Hadn't he told her on more than one occasion that she needed to let him do his job? Well, she would need to make sure he did the same. She wouldn't let anything happen to him. If he was willing to put himself at risk, she couldn't do anything less to protect him.

"Hello, Naya," Boris said as he joined her outside.

"Boris. Everything is going well inside."

"Very much so. Do you have a moment to talk?"

She nodded for him to continue.

"I see you brought another guard with you today."

"Yes. I thought it made sense to have a little extra security, and I can't initiate a portal gate without a device."

"That's what I wanted to discuss with you. If I gave you the portal device I have, would you be able to use it?"

"I should be able to, yes. Are you sure, though? Your clan would be at a disadvantage."

"You sacrificed your own device to protect my clan. It is only fair for you to have ours. Plus, it is my hope that eventually the realm will not separate the clans."

"Thank you."

"Since the doctors are busy with the realm demons today, they probably won't be able to implant the device until tomorrow. Mother has insisted that you come stay with her tonight."

"I would be honored to spend time with Irina."

Boris held open the door, and they both went back inside the warehouse.

"Are you ready to return?" Marrick asked when she rejoined him.

"I'll be staying overnight here. They have found a portal device I can use."

"Good. It will make things much easier, since we'll be linked again. I don't like not knowing where you are."

Naya grinned. "You are turning into a worrier, Marrick."

"Someone needs to worry about you," he responded with a grin of his own. He reached out and they grasped hands quickly before he opened a portal and stepped through.

As the gate closed, she felt eyes on her, and she turned to find Aleksei watching her intently. If she didn't know better, she would say his narrowed gaze and tight lips meant he was angry.

It reminded her of when they first met. There would be no arguing like before. If he planned to come with her to the realm, he would need to concede that she was in charge. She would not budge on that.

CHAPTER 18

Aleksei looked around the conference room table. With Boris, Irina, Doyle, Callie, the BSR team of Misha, Kyle, Jean Luc, Talia, and of course, Naya, all the seats were filled.

Everyone was tired after today's hectic pace, but he had still insisted on a quick wrap-up meeting to ensure issues were addressed while still fresh on everyone's mind. Overall, the list so far was minor.

"You guys rocked it, today," Kyle said.

Aleksei smiled. "I'm going to write this down in my calendar. On this day, Kyle McKinley gave me a compliment. Unless you were only referring to Doyle and Callie?"

"Ha, ha. I give praise when it's due."

"Well, I want to thank everyone here for all the hard work you've been putting in and will continue to put in," Aleksei said. "This would not have been possible without every one of you. Before we call it a night, I have one more item to discuss. Even after successfully bringing the next group to earth today, Naya has told me there are still issues in the realm. They don't trust us, and can we really blame them? We expect them to take our word after centuries of imprisonment. We tell them everything is better on earth, but we don't do anything to show them."

"Then what do you suggest, son?" Boris asked.

"I think we need to meet with the realm demons to show them we're serious. Have a spokesperson go to them."

"And who do you think should be this spokesperson?" Misha asked.

"I think it should be me. I'm heading up this program, so shouldn't I be the one to put a little skin in the game?"

Silence.

"Don't everyone agree at once," Aleksei said.

Kyle narrowed her eyes on him for a moment, and he braced himself for some sarcastic commentary. "I actually think it's a great idea."

"I agree," his babushka chimed in. "But who will help Callie and Doyle while you're gone?"

"I actually invited someone to pitch in while I'm away. She should have been here already."

As if in answer, the conference room door opened, and Sylvia walked in. "Hello! Sorry I'm running late. Did I miss the big announcement?"

"I just told them." Aleksei stood and offered her his seat. "Sylvia has graciously offered to help while I'm in the realm. With her expertise gained from helping the realm demons who were victims of the demon trafficking, she should have no trouble filling my shoes."

"I don't know if I have your gift for BS, Aleksei, but I'll do my best."

Everyone chuckled, and they spent a few minutes discussing other matters before he called the meeting to a close.

He wanted to speak to Naya, but Irina and Kyle took her with them, declaring they were having a girl's night. Misha and Callie walked out together, holding hands, followed by Jean Luc and Talia. Doyle and Sylvia left while discussing some ideas Sylvia had for the next immigration.

Which left Boris and Aleksei.

Aleksei wasn't sure what his father wanted to say, but from his tight expression, it was serious.

"Is there something wrong? You were unusually quiet after I announced my plan to go to the realm."

"Nothing is wrong. I stayed to tell you how proud I am of you."

Aleksei gaped at him.

"I've always known you have the ability to lead, but in the last few weeks you have shown all of us what the next leader of this clan looks like."

Aleksei shook his head. "My powers—"

"Are just one aspect of your leadership skills, Aleksei. I will review the clan laws to see how to revise this antiquated rule. Then I'll speak to the elders."

Aleksei cleared his throat. "Thank you."

"Will you leave tomorrow with Naya once she has the device implanted?"

"Yes."

"Come, then. Let's have a drink before you leave for the realm. I have some vodka I've been saving for the right occasion."

Boris clapped him on the back before they went to toast a successful day with some truly special vodka.

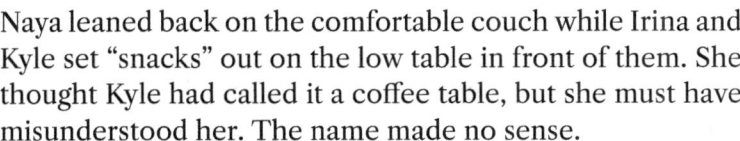

Naya leaned back on the comfortable couch while Irina and Kyle set "snacks" out on the low table in front of them. She thought Kyle had called it a coffee table, but she must have misunderstood her. The name made no sense.

The now-familiar bell rang, signaling that someone was at the door. Irina opened her front door to find Callie and Misha.

Irina wagged her finger at her grandson. "Mikhail, you can't stay. It's girl's night."

"I know, Babushka. I just want to say hi, and then I'll leave. I'm taking care of the twins tonight."

Kyle laughed. "Do you have Callie's number on speed dial?"

Misha scowled at her. "We will be fine. I'm more worried about you all behaving tonight." He looked over at Naya. "Can I count on you to keep these ladies under control?"

Naya smiled. "I have done much as a portal guard, but even I have my limits."

Misha's chuckle turned into a deep belly laugh. "It looks like they may have corrupted you already." He clapped his hands together. "Have fun, but not too much fun, ladies." He leaned down and kissed Callie on the lips.

Naya gaped at them. She had seen Misha hovering over Callie at the warehouse today, but she didn't realize it had progressed this far.

After the front door closed, Naya narrowed her eyes on Callie. "When were you going to tell me about this?"

Callie's cheeks turned pink. "It happened after you went back to the realm."

"Yep," Kyle said. "Irina had to stage an intervention."

Naya tilted her head. "What is an intervention?"

"I gathered our family and friends together to talk some sense into him," Irina replied.

"It took all of us to get the big doofus to admit he loved her," Kyle said.

Callie's face reddened further. "And then I told him a few things myself."

"It was epic!" Kyle exclaimed.

Naya chuckled. "I'm sorry I missed it."

Callie sat down next to her. "I want to thank you for the pep talk you gave me. You were right, I had to believe I'm worthy of love before I could let someone close."

Kyle sat down in a chair. "Okay. We need to change the subject or I'm going to get weepy, and you know how I hate getting weepy."

Callie clapped her hands together. "Fine. No weeping allowed tonight. We had such a good day today. We've already set a tentative date for the next group to come in two months. I think Aleksei's idea to visit the realm makes a lot of sense."

"Naya, what do you think?" Kyle asked. "You two haven't always seen eye to eye on things."

"He will need to be willing to listen to me. But I agree. It makes sense to have someone from earth meet with the realm clan leaders. And he is correct that it needs to be someone who is in a position of authority."

"Aleksei has no trouble bossing people around," Kyle said.

Irina smiled. "The way you two squabble, you really are like brother and sister."

"He's starting to grow on me, just like Misha did. But they are different, for sure."

Irina pursed her lips. "On the surface they seem different, but they both will do anything for the ones they love." She looked at Naya for a moment before standing. "Now, who would like a drink? It's time to get this girl's night started."

Naya happily followed the females into the kitchen. It was hard to believe that by this time tomorrow, Aleksei would be in Naya's world. They would be spending a considerable amount of time together. A thought that had her heart beating faster with trepidation...or was it anticipation?

CHAPTER 19

Aleksei hiked the strap of the small duffel up over his shoulder. It was time to put this plan in motion. He'd chosen to wear cargo pants, a long sleeve Henley shirt, fleece jacket, and hiking boots. Naya had given him instructions for how to dress after he rejected the idea of wearing a jumpsuit and armor. How could he represent what earth had to offer if he met the realm clan leaders dressed like a guard?

But it also paid to be prepared. His clothes fit loosely on his human form, so he had room to change to demon if need be. The last thing he needed was a torn-shirt-Incredible-Hulk moment in the realm.

He had already said goodbye to his babushka and father this morning. Misha, Kyle, and Jean Luc had come to see them off as well.

Misha grinned at him. "Good luck, brother."

"Yes, Aleksei," Kyle said, giving him a poke with her elbow. "Don't be your normal, charming self, or you'll start a coup."

Aleksei sighed. "I will endeavor to do my best, dear *sestra.*"

Naya activated the portal, and Aleksei stepped through it. Or more like, he was sucked in like quicksand. The light surrounded him until he had trouble breathing, and then quickly spit him out. He wobbled slightly when they came to a stop.

Naya held her staff in front of her as if braced for a fight, even though no one was nearby. He looked around. The ground was barren except for red crystalline rocks peppering the landscape. The sky was a faded bluish gray.

"This is our desert. Farther south are caves made out of the red rocks you see here. We'll go west for a short distance to reach the jump point to the in-between. It will be dark soon, and we don't want to be in the realm alone at night."

They started walking.

"It was midafternoon when we left earth. How different is the time here?"

"Our time moves much faster. What seems to be a few hours on earth can equate to a day here."

"So in earth terms, you returned to the realm a week ago."

"I actually spent more than a month back in the realm."

Aleksei rubbed his hand over his face. "I knew there was a time difference, but I didn't realize it was major. This means the months it takes us to organize a relocation equates to close to a year of waiting."

"Yes."

He nodded. "Is it this barren everywhere?"

"No. We have forest lands, as well as fields where we grow food. There are also streams, and two large lakes."

Naya tensed next to him, and he followed her gaze to an outcropping of larger crystals. A demon stood on top of one of the crystals watching them, and from his green and brown skin tone, he was a Dragan demon. They could control heat and flame. The elders on earth believed they might have been the inspiration for the dragon myths that fascinate humans.

"We will continue on our way," Naya said softly. "He is not making any moves to attack us. I think he's more curious about seeing you in your human form."

"Fine with me. If news of my arrival starts to spread, it can only be beneficial for our cause."

They walked a few more minutes until they reached a dry creek bed. Naya looked around carefully before activating another gate. They stepped through, and after feeling like he was breathing pudding, they ended up in a field of ankle-high grass.

Naya pointed to the left. "Do you see the smoke? That's the portal guard village."

They strode through the grass at a fast clip, arriving at the village of small huts in less than ten minutes. Aleksei wasn't surprised to see Marrick there to greet them. The large Pavel demon grasped both of Naya's arms. It was obviously their sign of greeting, but Aleksei thought Marrick held on a little too long.

"Has everything been relatively quiet since last time we communicated?" Naya asked.

"Yes. I spent the last couple days spreading the word about a representative from earth coming to meet with the clan leaders."

"Excellent," Aleksei said. "Who do you think we should visit first? Maybe someone who might be more willing to listen to what I have to say? If we can win over one of the leaders, it would help with later discussions with the more difficult ones."

Marrick's expression brightened. "Naya and I have reached the same conclusion. I think we should start with Colan, the Palthat leader. He may be willing to listen to what we have to say."

Naya held up her hand. "Why don't we discuss strategy over dinner?"

Marrick nodded. "Very well. I need to debrief some of the guards who just returned from patrol anyway. I'll join you in an hour."

Naya beckoned for Aleksei to follow her to a small hut with a thatched roof, where she opened the door and walked in, and Aleksei joined her, quickly scanning the room. There was a cold fireplace with a pot suspended on a metal hook. Next to the fireplace sat a small table with two chairs. A set of shelves held various pieces of pottery, and a door led to a room with a bed and a small bedside stand. In the corner of the main room sat stacks and stacks of books. Aleksei walked over to the books and read the spines. He was surprised at the diversity of authors.

"You obviously love to read." A small duffel sat on the floor. Several books were stacked inside. "So this is what Kyle has been giving you."

"Yes. She feeds my obsession with stories."

"May I?" Aleksei asked.

Naya nodded, and he picked up a book from one of the stacks. *Little Women* by Louisa May Alcott.

"You probably find it silly."

Aleksei ran his fingers over the leather cover. "Not at all. I can understand why you would want to escape into these other worlds. I used to read a lot too."

"Why did you stop?"

"I started reading books about businesses and leadership."

"Sounds boring."

Aleksei chuckled at her bluntness. "Pretty much. What can I do to help you with dinner?"

Her eyebrows rose. "You can cook?"

"Why does it surprise you? I live on my own. If I couldn't cook for myself, I would have to eat at restaurants all the time."

"Callie told me about restaurants. I can't believe there are actually places that prepare and serve food."

"Now that you can maintain your human form, when we go back to earth I'll take you to any restaurant you want."

What the hell was he doing? It was like he was asking her on a date.

"You can put your bag down by the door and help me prepare dinner. If we don't start soon, the food won't be ready by the time Marrick arrives."

Aleksei nodded. Marrick. How could he ask her about their relationship without asking about their relationship? And why did he care? He had already explained his fifty-year plan to Naya, and she hadn't batted an eye. He was the one who couldn't get her out of his mind. Maybe she had been so accepting of what he said because she was already in a relationship with Marrick? Had she simply kissed him out of curiosity?

She removed her armor and hung it on a hook by the door. She was gorgeous, but he missed seeing her in jeans and a blouse. Here, she never truly got to relax. None of the guard did. He pulled out the small notebook from his jacket pocket and wrote a couple lines.

"What are you doing?" Naya asked as she knelt down to start the fire.

"I'm making a note to talk to the guards about what they want to do once the immigration is complete. The realm demons aren't the only ones who will need to be acclimated to earth." He tucked the notebook back in his pocket. "Have you thought about what you want to do?"

She concentrated for a moment on the fire before standing once a small flame erupted. "I haven't let myself think that far in advance."

"Well, now the relocations have begun, you might want to start figuring out what you want to do."

She frowned slightly for a moment before reaching for a bowl with what looked like potatoes, although the skins were light blue. "I've never had a reason to plan ahead. We live in the moment here."

Damn. The clans on earth had a lot to make up for. He cleared his throat to gather his thoughts. "If I have my way, that will change for you."

She cut the vegetables into chunks and dropped them into the pot hanging above the fire. "I can't imagine you without a plan in place."

He shrugged. "I can be a bit too detailed, but I think it's been an asset with the immigration plans."

"I wouldn't have agreed when I first met you."

"Now?"

"Now, I would say there are pluses to being organized."

"I'll take that as a compliment. Now tell me how I can help with dinner."

They stood side by side, slicing vegetables and placing them in the pot as the liquid slowly started to boil. Naya sprinkled some sort of spice in the pot, and a smoky aroma filled the small space.

She looked over at him. He couldn't stop himself from reaching out and tucking a loose strand of hair behind her ear.

Alarm bells went off in his brain. This was not part of his plan. He was here in the realm for a reason, and it wasn't standing in front of him. He leaned toward her. It wasn't standing—

A knock at the door had them each taking a step back. Naya walked around him and opened the door for Marrick. He should have known.

"Are we ready to make some plans?" Marrick asked.

Aleksei watched Naya return to the fire. For the first time in recent memory, the last thing Aleksei wanted to do right now was make plans.

CHAPTER 20

Naya strode toward the forest with Aleksei and Marrick following behind her, deep in conversation. Had they not talked enough last night? Naya hadn't realized how much the two males were alike until they sat at the small table for several hours discussing the best ways to approach the Palthat.

She kept a vigilant watch on the upcoming trees to make sure there were no surprises. At least *she* was watching for danger while the other two chatted.

"Remember to acknowledge the leader first before addressing the rest of the clan," Marrick said.

"Haven't you two gone over this enough?" Naya asked.

"It never hurts to review things more than once," Aleksei said.

"Now that we're entering the forest, it might be a good idea to be a little less talkative and a little more aware of your surroundings."

For a moment she thought he was going to argue with her, but then he surprised her by nodding. Marrick took point as they wound through the trees, heading east toward the Palthat village just beyond the edge of the forest.

"This forest is massive," Aleksei commented after they'd been hiking for an hour.

Marrick pointed to his right. "We're traveling the northern edge, which is actually the narrow part of the forest. Farther south, the forest expands and is far more dense. The Kelmar live just past the forest in the southern crystal caves."

"We expect resistance from them," Aleksei said, framing it more like a statement then a question.

Naya hopped over a fallen tree. "The Kelmar have resisted the relocation since the beginning. If we can convince the other four clans we're sincere, it will go a long way toward convincing the Kelmar."

Marrick held up his hand, and they both stopped and fell silent.

"We're close to the village. We should be meeting their sentries soon."

Naya tightened the grip on her staff. Aleksei was willing to risk his life to bring the realm demons to earth. She could do no less. She would protect him with her life.

Marrick emerged slowly from the protection of the trees. As they had anticipated, ahead of them waited two sentries. One carried a spear, the other a sword.

Aleksei stepped forward and spoke in demon tongue. "I am here to see Colan."

"You are an earther," the larger demon said.

"Yes. Will you take my request to Colan to see if he will agree to meet with me?" Aleksei asked in a calm voice.

The two looked at each other, and the smaller demon turned and trotted toward the smoke curling in the distance. The village was over the small rise. They waited in silence until the demon returned and beckoned for them to follow.

They reached the village center, where the clan apparently gathered for events. A fire burned in a large ring, and the Palthat leader awaited them in front of the fire, with his clan members on either side of him. Clan members with pale blue skin who were glaring at both her and Marrick.

Aleksei stopped at the edge of the clearing. "You both should wait here."

"That is not a good idea," Naya said.

"If you come with me, looking all dangerous and intimidating, it will be harder to get them to trust me. Let me do this. I know you'll swoop in with your trusty staff if something goes wrong."

She scowled at him. "Very well, but I promised Irina I would protect you."

He grinned in response. "And we don't want you to face Babushka's wrath."

He walked into the village, and she clutched her staff, moving slightly so she could see Aleksei's profile. While Colan watched him approach alone, he appeared to relax, which in turn spread like a wave through the clan. Aleksei stopped several feet from them, but with their demon hearing she and Marrick would be able to listen to the conversation.

Aleksei inclined his head in greeting and spoke in demon tongue. "Thank you for meeting with me. My name is Aleksei, and I'm responsible for helping bring you to earth if you want to move there."

Colan looked Aleksei's human form up and down. "So you actually came to the realm. I thought earther demons were scared of the barbarians locked away here."

"I'm sorry it's taken so long for me to come meet you, and I don't believe you're barbarians."

"Then why do you travel with the guard as protection?"

"I don't know my way around the realm. These guards have agreed to take me to the clan villages so I may meet with the leaders."

"And what is it you want to discuss with us?"

"I understand there has been resistance to the relocation to earth."

Colan crossed his arms. "Can you blame us for being hesitant?"

"Absolutely not. If I were in your position I would feel the same. You and your ancestors have spent centuries living here as prisoners. Now we come from earth and egotistically announce we're here to save you. You can argue there's nothing to save you from."

Colan's eyebrows hiked up at Aleksei's straightforward approach. "And what do you hope your visit to the realm will accomplish?"

"I want to meet and talk with the various clans so I can understand what it is *you* want. If there are clan members who wish to stay in the realm, they should be allowed to do so. But before any of you make a decision, I have come to see what assurances you need from me if you do decide to come to earth."

Murmurs rippled through the clan until Colan held up his hand and they all went silent. "We want to see the demon we are dealing with before any discussions continue."

Aleksei nodded and set his demon form free so his body grew and filled out the loose clothes he wore. His skin changed to orange with red markings across his face and hands. Naya had seen Misha change similarly, but Aleksei exuded a barely-contained power in demon form that she hadn't noticed in Misha.

He was a male who should not be challenged. Except for her. She felt an overwhelming need to be the one to challenge him.

Colan stared at Aleksei for several drawn-out seconds before nodding.

Naya let out the breath she'd been holding.

An hour later, Marrick and Naya still stood on the edge of the clearing watching Colan and Aleksei chat as if they were old friends. Aleksei was amazing. He had known honesty would be the only thing that would work with the Palthat.

Aleksei's head fell back while he laughed at something the clan leader said. She watched him in awe. She'd never heard him laugh that way before.

"You have feelings for him," Marrick said softly.

She looked up at him. "What?"

"We have been friends since childhood, Naya. I can see it in your eyes. You care for him."

"It doesn't matter," she said, sounding defeated even to her own ears.

"How can you say that?"

"I'm not part of the plans he has for his life."

"He told you this?" Marrick asked with a growl.

"Yes. Not in a cruel manner. He was being honest. He has plans," she said again as if the repetition would somehow make it more convincing.

Marrick snorted. "Since when has anyone's plans stopped you before?"

Naya barely managed a smile. "It might have been true in the past."

"And what has changed to make you hesitant now?"

Naya didn't respond, the lump in her throat blocking the words.

"Ah," Marrick said, then went silent.

Ah? What did he mean? "Are you not going to explain yourself?" Naya asked.

"You have never been scared to voice your opinion, my dearest friend. Except when it comes to your heart. You are using his plans as a feeble excuse to avoid telling him how you feel."

Anger flared in her chest. "He doesn't feel the same way."

"You don't know that. Males are clueless when it comes to emotions. Sometimes we have to be pummeled over the head before we realize the truth."

Like the intervention Irina staged for Misha. Could she plan her own intervention?

Marrick looked down at her. "Think of it this way. Which is worse? Talking to Aleksei and finding out he doesn't share your feelings, or never admitting it to him and wondering if you could have been happy together?"

For a moment she couldn't decide which was worse. But hadn't she been trying to get Aleksei to stop thinking things through so much? And yet here she was, paralyzed by her doubts.

It was time to take a leap again. She would know the truth, one way or the other. But at least she wouldn't always wonder *what if.*

CHAPTER 21

Aleksei could hear the Rocky theme song in his head. He wanted to throw his fists in the air and do a victory dance. Since neither Naya nor Marrick would get the reference, he walked alongside them instead. They had just passed through the portal, his lungs feeling like they had been wrung out like a wet towel, before landing in the field that led to the portal guard village in the in-between.

One clan down, four to go. Although he wasn't about to get cocky. Hopefully the next clan meeting would go as well. Colan had even suggested that Aleksei introduce himself to the Dragan clan leader next. Apparently, he found him to be reasonable. Aleksei could handle reasonable.

"Do you agree with Colan about approaching the Dragans next?" Aleksei asked Marrick, since Naya had been quiet since leaving the village. Was she still upset with him for making them stand back during the conversation with the clan leader?

"Yes. I'm sure word is already spreading of your meeting with the Palthats. It makes sense to visit with the Dragans next. Those two clans have gotten along relatively well over the centuries."

"Tell me more about their clan."

Marrick spent the rest of the way to the huts describing the Dragans, with Aleksei asking questions at appropriate times. But the longer they walked and Naya held her tongue, the more worried Aleksei became. Was she sick? He wanted to ask her if she was all right, but he didn't think she would appreciate him exhibiting concern in front of Marrick.

They arrived at Naya's hut twenty minutes later, and Marrick stopped at the door instead of coming inside.

"I am going to do some rounds and check on the other guards," he said. "You know where my hut is, Aleksei. Feel free to sleep there again tonight if you like."

Aleksei shook his hand. "Thank you for your help today."

Marrick said his goodnights to Naya and walked away. When they entered the hut, Naya immediately pulled her armor off and hung it by the door. Then she changed into her human form, and he studied her as he turned back to human as well.

"It must be nice to be able to take your armor off after wearing it all day."

Naya shrugged. "I'm used to it." She walked over to the fireplace and squatted down to start the fire.

Aleksei couldn't stand her silence any longer. "Is something wrong?"

She didn't respond immediately, instead making sure the fire took before standing and facing him. "Nothing is wrong. I've been thinking about some things. My future."

"Really?"

"Yes. I might not have a fifty-year plan like you do, but I have decided what I want to do now." She took a step closer. "And who I want to do it with."

He gulped—actually gulped—the sound loud in the small hut. She smiled at him, and her satisfied grin had him crossing the rest of the way to her.

"I know you said you didn't see our relationship being long term, but I have decided I still want to be with you for whatever time I can have. If you want me?" Naya asked.

Holy Fates, he wanted her more than his next breath. "I've been having trouble not touching you. I can't wait to feel you against me."

She reached for him, and he grabbed her wrist to stop her.

"What about Marrick?" Aleksei asked.

Naya tilted her head and looked at him. "What about him?"

"What is he to you?"

"He is my second-in-charge and best friend."

"And?"

"And he is loyal, and honorable, and would die for me, as I would for him."

"When did this discussion turn into a celebration of Marrick?" Aleksei growled.

She shrugged. "You brought Marrick up. I was answer—"

He placed his fingers over her lips. "Enough about him. I am going to kiss you now, Naya. I can't wait anym—"

She surged forward and locked her lips to his. He wrapped his arms around her, and pulled her close, tasting her. She was only a couple of inches shorter than he was, and they fit together perfectly.

Naya ran her fingers through his hair, and he clutched her tighter to him. He needed to calm the hell down. He was acting like a randy teenager, but when was the last time he had felt this way about any female?

He ran his mouth along her jawline and kissed her behind her ear before he sucked her lobe into his mouth. When she whimpered he almost spilled in his pants. *Damn.*

He took a step back and gazed into her dark brown eyes. They looked sleepy, heavy-lidded, and sexy as all hell. But he needed to set some ground rules. She had said she was okay in the moment, but he had to be certain, even though his body was screaming at him to shut the hell up.

"Are you sure, Naya? I can't promise a long-term relationship."

"I know. I just want to feel something besides the armor weighing down my skin and bones and the constant need to be on the lookout. Never relaxing."

He placed his hands gently on each side of her face. "I'll do whatever I can to lift the weight off you. But I will tell you there will be no relaxing in the near future. If there is, I'm doing something wrong."

Naya laughed, and her eyes lit up from within. He gaped at her. He'd never seen her laugh before. She needed a life full of laughter.

"I never thought you would leave your fancy suits behind, but I like this Aleksei."

He winked at her. "So you've been thinking about me without my clothes on?"

Her cheeks darkened, and he rubbed his thumbs over them. "I have my own confession to make. Ever since you told me you sleep naked, I haven't been able to stop imagining what you look like."

"Is it so strange to sleep naked? Everyone seems worried about it."

"Who's everyone?" he growled. "Who have you been telling that you sleep naked?"

"Just Irina and Kyle." She leaned forward and rested her forehead against his. "Are you jealous, Aleksei Chesnokov? You sound jealous to me."

His heart ricocheted around his chest. He didn't respond with words, instead choosing to show her how he felt instead. He kissed her again, this time trying to own her, devour her with his mouth. He worried for a moment that he was being too rough, until she wrapped her arms around him, pulled him closer, and tangled her tongue with his.

After a few more minutes, they wrenched apart, both gasping in air. Naya shoved his jacket off and then ran her hands under his shirt. He jerked as her warm fingers drew a path up his chest. She helped him pull the shirt up and off, and she tilted her head while she examined him intently.

"I watched you running in the training center, your shirt sticking to your back, and I knew you were beautiful."

He reached for her, then stopped. "How do I get you out of this thing?"

She laughed again—damn, he loved the sound—and she pushed a flap up and revealed clasps down the front of her jumpsuit. Aleksei watched her fingers intently as she slowly opened each clasp. He held his breath as she pulled open the suit and let it drop to the floor.

Holy Fates...Holy Hell...Holy—

She was naked, and so amazing he blinked to make sure she wasn't a mirage. Her legs went on for miles, with a flat stomach, and breasts exactly the right size to fill his hands. He had known she would be an Amazon warrior, and this confirmed it.

His hands shook as he reached for her and ran his fingers along her bare arms. Her skin was soft and warm, and he leaned in to kiss her again. They both moaned when their skin touched. Naya held out her hand, and he took it, letting her pull him into the bedroom.

"I don't think things will progress if you don't remove your pants," Naya said with a smirk.

He kicked off his boots, yanked his socks off, and pushed down his pants and boxers before stepping out of them.

Naya's eyebrows rose—his ego assured him it was in appreciation—and she reached for him, pushing him so he sat and then lay down on the bed.

Oh, he was so going to love this.

She crawled up his body and kissed him before moving her lips down his throat and onto his chest. He moaned as she headed south, and then groaned loudly when she reached her destination. This female was made for him.

Within minutes he was having trouble controlling himself, but he was not about to let things end this way. He reached for her arms and pulled her up his body until she lay on top of his chest, which did *not* calm him down. At all.

He wrapped his hand around the back of her head, but he couldn't run his fingers through her gorgeous hair. Aleksei traced his hand down her braid, pulled the tie off, and unwound the long plait to run his fingers through her long, silky hair.

She sat up, her hair cascading around her shoulders. The sight almost made him weep. He lifted her hips, helping her to settle on him, and they moaned as they joined together. She leaned down and gave him a drawn-out kiss before starting to move.

His eyes closed for a moment, the sensation too intense, but he fought to keep them open. There was too much to see, from her skin to the wonder in her eyes as she grew closer to the brink. Slow turned fast, sighs became pants, and he gritted his teeth to hold on until she tumbled first. When she shuddered, he let go with her, closing his eyes at the sparks that filled his vision.

Naya collapsed onto his chest, and he wrapped his arms around her. "I don't have words to describe what just happened," he murmured as he nuzzled her neck.

She set her chin on his chest so she could look him in the eyes. "You? No words? I can't believe it."

He smiled at her. "Are you saying I talk too much?"

She nodded, her chin rubbing across his chest. "You do like to talk a lot. I would think your tongue would be tired most of the time."

She gasped as he flipped her under him. "You should be happy I like to talk, because it means my tongue gets lots of exercise. Let me show you what I can do with this talented tongue."

And before she could protest, he did.

Twice.

CHAPTER 22

Naya woke up against a warm body, her head resting on Aleksei's shoulder. It hadn't been a dream. And he was still with her, his arm wrapped around her.

She watched him sleep for a few minutes. He looked different when the weight of the world wasn't resting on his shoulders. Younger.

"Are you watching me while I sleep?" he mumbled as his green eyes flicked open.

Heat ran along Naya's neck and face. She had never blushed this much before. She traced her finger over his mouth and along his jawline. "What do you think Irina would say if she knew I seduced you?"

Aleksei ran his hand lightly along her arm. "I think she would get a kick out of it. She is always poking her nose—I mean, looking out for everyone in the clan, but she is especially involved in her family's business."

"You are lucky to have such a supportive family."

"They do test my patience sometimes, because they can be *too* supportive, but I know how lucky I am." He rubbed her arms some more. "Will you tell me about your family?"

Naya hesitated. She never talked about her parents now they were gone, but it wasn't a secret. "My grandparents volunteered to become portal guards, and they served until they passed. My parents were both born in the in-between and took up the calling as well. They were a good match.

My father was from the Pavel clan, and my mother, Shamat. They mated and fought alongside each other for centuries. When I was born, my mother wanted to leave the in-between, but my father felt it was their duty to remain as portal guards."

She cleared her throat, and Aleksei stayed silent, as if he sensed this was hard for her to say. "As a child I overheard their disagreements, but I didn't understand what they were truly about until I was older. One night my mother was killed on patrol. I was in bed when the guard came to tell my father, but I heard their whispered words. And after they left I confronted my father." She closed her eyes and took a breath.

"I blamed him for her death. Told him if we had left the realm she would still be alive. I was horrible to him."

Aleksei lifted her chin and she stared into eyes filled with compassion. "How old were you when she died?"

"Fourteen."

"You were still a child, Naya."

She shook her head. "He was never the same after that night. Two years later he died as well. We found him at the bottom of a ravine, his neck broken. The guard assumed he had been attacked by a realm demon." She cleared her throat. "But a voice inside me has always wondered if he took his own life."

And if that was the truth of it, her father hadn't been strong enough to stay for her. His grief had overpowered the love he proclaimed he felt for her.

Aleksei pushed a stand of hair behind her ear. "You were on your own at sixteen?"

She shrugged. "I was old enough to fight."

He frowned. "Don't shrug like it was no big deal. It is a big deal, Naya. Why did you stay?"

Why had she stayed? Did she dare tell him she had nowhere to truly go? "It was my duty. And the guard is my family."

He closed his eyes for a moment, as if in pain. When he opened them again, his expression was hard with determination. "I will do everything I can to get the realm demons and guards to earth if it's what they want. We have to convince the clan leaders to at least listen and give earth a chance."

"You are a good male, Aleksei." She kissed his shoulder, and he placed his fingers under her chin and tilted her face up so he could kiss her softly on the lips.

"You are an amazing female, Naya."

She pulled him toward her, pressing her chest against his. How could her appetite for him not be quenched? But she wanted him even more than before, which scared her to death. She had assured him she did not expect a long-term relationship. Which meant she needed to live up to her promises, even if her heart protested loudly. What if she risked letting him close only to have him abandon her like her father had?

<hr />

Once again Naya and Marrick waited on the outskirts. Aleksei had introduced himself to the Dragan clan leader, who stared at him for several drawn-out moments before finally speaking.

"You are the earther who visited the Palthat."

"Yes. I'm here to discuss any concerns you and your clan might have about relocating to earth."

"How do we know what you tell us about earth is the truth?"

"A good question. What if I can have some of the realm demons who have already gone to earth come back and tell you what it's like there? You would believe them over an earther, correct?"

"Yes. You would let them come back here?"

"Of course. If they're willing." Aleksei pulled out his small notebook and pen. "I'll make a note of your request and set up some return trips so they can visit you. I will also see about bringing books to explain different things on earth as well."

Chatter burst out among the clan members sitting around the leader. Aleksei was winning them over.

The clan leader lifted his hand, and the chatter died away. "It is taking a long time to send small numbers to earth. If we have more who wish to come, can you not speed up the process?"

Aleksei tapped his pen against his notebook before responding. "Bringing in greater numbers is one of my priorities as well. We plan on bringing a group of forty or fifty to earth in two months, but that is earth time. I understand that here in the realm time passes much faster. A couple hours on earth can be a day in the realm. So two months for earth could be almost a year here."

The leader frowned. "That makes things harder."

"It does. I hope to eventually get to the point where we can bring one hundred demons at a time. But unlike the realm, we have to be concerned about exposure to humans. They don't know about supernaturals, and we must keep it that way so the human population won't panic. So it takes more time to acclimate realm demons to earth, starting with teaching you how to turn into your human form."

"I understand, but it's difficult for those who wish to leave to have to wait."

"Agreed. But right now I can't promise you I can bring everyone who wants to come as quickly as we all would wish." He tapped his pen again. "So what would help in the meantime?" He looked around the different clan members, drawing them in.

Naya was awestruck at how he handled this discussion. He had some of his father in him, but he was less of a showman, and sincere, which made him all the more powerful.

"From the rumors we hear of earth, it is much easier to survive there. From food to clothing to machinery that does magical things. Can we have some of those things now?"

Aleksei sat up and smiled. Naya sucked in her breath at the intensity.

"What a great idea. I can't help you with the magical things, since most of our machinery won't work here, but we can see about bringing other items from earth. Clothing and food, most definitely. We can sit down with the clans and put together a list of items we can transport to the realm. And not just for those who wish to come to earth. We can see about bringing items for the clan members who decide to stay here as well.

"You would do that?" he asked.

"Yes. I will reach out to my team on earth to get things started. We'll need to get someone to oversee this," he mumbled to himself while making notes in his small book. "Are there some things you can think of now that you would like?"

"I would like one of the warm shirts you have on."

Aleksei laughed, his eyes sparkling. "My jacket?" He took the coat off. "Here. Take this, and we'll see about sending more."

Aleksei handed it to the clan leader who pulled the coat on. Several clan members ran their hands over the soft fleece.

He grinned and held out his arm. "We will be willing to meet with you again, Aleksei."

Aleksei gripped his arm and grinned back at him. "Good. I'm glad your people are willing to give earth a chance. In the meantime, we'll see about sending you some items to make living here a little easier."

Several hours later, Naya, Marrick, and Aleksei ambled along the field leading to the guard village. They had been dissecting the most recent meeting on their trek back.

Marrick slapped Aleksei on the back. "Another successful discussion."

"Yes. But you heard what he said. There are still demons trying to stir up trouble here in the realm."

"From the description the clan leader gave us, it sounds like they are the two other demons who attacked the Shamat compound along with the Kelmar," Naya said.

"How do we stop them?"

"The clan we will visit next are the Lagfel. Maybe they can talk to their clan member and convince him to listen to us."

Marrick stopped at the edge of the village. "I am going to find the guards and ask them to do another sweep to look for our two rogue demons. Maybe we'll find them."

Naya nodded. "Let's plan on leaving for the Lagfel village in the morning. It's almost a day's walk from here, which will give us plenty of time to plan for Aleksei's meeting with the clan leader."

"That will work," Marrick said. He bowed slightly to Aleksei. "I'll see you in the morning."

Marrick smirked at her before walking away. She frowned.

"Is something wrong?" Aleksei asked.

"He is assuming you will spend the night with me again."

"I'm not?" he asked with his own smirk.

"Males," Naya muttered, as she stomped into her hut.

Aleksei followed her inside, grabbed her from behind, and kissed the side of her neck behind her ear. "I can always go back to Marrick's hut for the night."

She spun around in his arms, and he helped her pull her armor off, letting it drop onto the packed earth floor.

"You are very sure of yourself," she said, nipping at his chin.

He found the flap on her jumpsuit and quickly undid the fastenings, letting the jumpsuit hit the floor as well. Aleksei's gaze caressed her as he looked her up and down. Everywhere his gaze landed warmed as it would if he touched her.

She reached for his pants, fumbling for a second with the button and fastener, before reaching inside. Naya stroked him for a few moments until he pulled her hand away, pushed his pants down, and picked her up.

Pushing her back against the hut wall, he helped her wrap her legs around him right before he surged inside her. His mouth swallowed her groan before his tongue also surged into her mouth, synchronizing with the driving rhythm he maintained below.

Naya's nails gripped his shoulders, hard. Aleksei's rhythm increased until they both shot over the edge, and then clung to each other while Naya attempted to regain her equilibrium. Luckily, Aleksei kept her steady, or she would have slid down the wall to the floor.

Aleksei looked down at her. "Are you okay?"

She nodded, and his cocky grin appeared. "Good. Are you ready to take this to the bed?"

"Are you going to take your clothes off this time?"

He laughed. "If you undress me."

"Deal."

She held out her hand, and he wrapped his hand around hers before she pulled him toward the bedroom.

———◆◇◆———

Several hours later, Naya lay with Aleksei wrapped around her. She had never felt so content before. But she couldn't get too used to the feeling. Once Aleksei went home, this...whatever it was...would be over.

A hand ran along her spine. "What are you thinking about so hard?"

"I was wondering about your childhood. Will you tell me about it?"

He smiled. "I was lucky. I have a family who loves me. They butt into my business at times, but I have to remind myself that they do it because they care.

"My father didn't meet my mother until he was a little over five hundred. Babushka has told me he had given up on finding his true love, and then my mother showed up one day, and, according to Boris, he fell in love with her at first sight. Then he spent over a year wooing her before she would even agree to a date. Back then it would have required a meeting between families, since propriety wouldn't have allowed them to be alone together."

"Like in my historical novels."

"Exactly. My mother wanted to marry for love. Father brought her every bauble and trinket he could think of, but she refused him. He started to call on her, and would sit with her for hours in the gardens at her parents' estate in Russia. This was prior to the fall, when families still had riches. When her family lost their money, my father was the only suitor who continued to pursue her. It was never about the money for him, only her. And that's when she said yes."

"Misha is the oldest."

"Yes. He is fifteen years older than I am. He was born while the clan still lived in Russia. I was born a couple years after the clan moved into Europe for several decades before finally raising enough money to sail to America. My father wanted us to find a place to thrive."

"What about your younger brother?"

Aleksei's eyes lost some of their joy. "Sergei is five years younger than me, so, unlike with Misha, we grew up together. My mother adored him. He was the baby, and she spoiled him. After our mother died, Sergei withdrew from everyone. When he was old enough, he left our clan to find his own way, whatever the hell that means. It practically destroyed my father. First he lost his wife, and then his son."

"And you lost a brother."

Aleksei nodded. "I love Misha, but he was an adult and had moved away when I was still young. With Sergei, I..."

"Shared a childhood with him."

"Exactly. When we were growing up, I felt like I needed to protect him. Not just because I'm his older brother, but because Sergei never developed any powers. As far as I know, he can't turn into his demon form, either."

Naya gaped at him before schooling her features. "I've never heard of that before."

"I don't imagine a demon born in the realm would survive long without powers. It's extremely rare on earth, but it does happen."

"When is the last time you spoke to him?" she asked.

"Two years ago. It was the last time he came for a visit. We had a fight. I told him he was wasting his life. Looking back at it, I can see I was being a pompous ass."

"I can hardly imagine," Naya said, widening her eyes in fake shock.

Aleksei barked out a laugh. "You've experienced it first-hand."

"So I have. But now that I know you, I know it's because you want the best for everyone. That does not make you an ass."

"What about pompous?"

She chuckled. "That you need to work on."

He placed both hands on her face and pulled her in for a kiss. "I don't know what I'm going to do with you, Naya."

She kissed down his chin and nibbled along his neck. "I have some ideas."

He sucked in a breath. "Feel free to elaborate."

Naya winked before she headed south.

CHAPTER 23

They walked for several hours before they arrived at a small set of foothills. Even after running on the treadmill every day, Aleksei was tired. He watched both Naya and Marrick stride along in front of him as if they had an inexhaustible energy supply.

It didn't help that he had gotten little sleep the previous night. Making love to Naya was amazing. He didn't regret it, even though it meant dragging his feet today. Naya strode along with power and grace. Her staff always at the ready, and she was a demon he couldn't help but take seriously. The more time he spent with her, the more he wanted to get to know her—all of her, because he had a feeling she hid her emotions behind a protective barrier as strong as the armor she used to protect her body. Once he had met with all the clans, he wanted to spend more time with her.

Which meant it was important to have a successful meeting with the Lagfel. If he could convince them to listen, the Bureau would be another step closer to containing the protests. Naya had distracted him last night, and before either of them got distracted tonight he would have her reach out to Kyle with her telepathy. Kyle could talk to Callie and Doyle about collecting and sending supplies here. Even if he could initially collect only a small number of requested items, it would show his sincerity. He needed to back up his talk with action.

Marrick held up his hand, and they stopped. "The village is not far from here. Any questions before the sentries arrive?"

Aleksei shook his head. "I'm ready. We know this is probably going to be a harder sell since one of the clan has been attempting to stop the immigration. Hopefully word has spread from my meetings with the other clans."

Neither had a chance to respond, since three gray demons walked toward them, each carrying a weapon similar to the large scythe the demon had carried when he attacked the Shamat compound.

Marrick and Naya tensed, and Aleksei didn't blame them. The sentries were not happy to see them.

"I am—"

"We know who you are, earther," the middle demon growled.

"Then you know I am here to see your leader."

Scowls passed among the three Lagfel before the middle spoke again. "Come with us."

They walked another ten minutes before they reached the Lagfel village. As they approached the village center, demons emerged from their huts and followed them. Unlike the previous two villages, the demons here looked at them with suspicion more than curiosity.

The sentries stopped in front of one of the largest demons Aleksei had ever seen.

"I wondered when you would get here to spread your lies."

Aleksei groaned on the inside. He had his work cut out for him. "I am here to answer your questions about earth and the demon immigration. I understand words mean little if not backed up with action. So let's discuss what I can do for you."

"We have been told that our people are being turned into slaves on earth."

Aleksei looked the clan leader straight in the eye. "The two groups I have helped bring to earth are not slaves. We did discover that some of the Abstatholm here in the realm were bringing demons to earth and forcing them into slavery. The guard we have on earth discovered this was happening and freed those realm demons, which is why we have created this immigration program. We want the realm demons to be able to come to earth freely."

"You will allow us to speak to the Lagfel who have already moved to earth?"

So he'd already heard about Aleksei's earlier conversation with the other two clans. "Yes. I know one of the first group of five who emigrated there was a Lagfel." Aleksei had made a point of bringing one of each clan in the first group to show they would all be treated equally. "And there were five in the second group of twenty who arrived this week. I will speak to them and have one return to tell you of their experiences so far."

"We have been told you abuse our people."

Aleksei gritted his teeth. "No one is abusing the realm demons. If anyone lays a finger on them, they will answer to me. Can I ask you a question?"

"Yes."

"These are all serious accusations. Where have they come from? How have you learned of them?"

"One of my clan has been to earth. He has seen things."

"Has he given you proof?" Aleksei asked.

His eyes narrowed.

Aleksei continued. "As I said earlier, words need to be backed up with actions."

"Are you saying my clansman is lying?"

"I am saying that before you throw away your clan's chance to come to earth and start a better life, you should let me prove these accusations are false."

Aleksei had once again calmed the clan leader. He was truly gifted, but she couldn't tell him so too many times, or his ego would get even bigger. Naya watched the other clan members carefully, to see if she recognized the demon who had attacked the Shamat compound.

A demon on the outskirts caught her eye. He had become more and more agitated, the longer Aleksei and the leader conversed. Naya reached out to Marrick through their telepathic link.

"Marrick. I think I see the demon we've been looking for. I'm going to get closer, follow him if necessary."

"Let me do it."

"No. I want you to protect Aleksei. I'll be careful."

"If you leave, report in every thirty minutes."

She nodded. *"Of course I will follow protocol, overprotective male."*

Naya skirted along the edge of the crowd. Once she was closer to the demon, she confirmed her suspicions. He was the one who had attacked the compound along with the Majock and Kelmar. He backed away, shoving through the crowd.

Naya followed, attempting to stay far enough back that he wouldn't see her. But she knew it wouldn't last long if he left the village. She could hide for a bit in the foothills, but after that they would be in wide-open fields. The demon jogged past the last house and headed down the path toward the first hill. Naya waited as long as she dared for fear of losing him, and then hurried toward the hill.

Marrick. I'm following him. I want to see if he leads me to the Majock or anyone else involved in the attacks.

Are you sure you want to do this alone?

Aleksei is doing his part. Now it's my turn to help.

Be careful.

She continued for several minutes, staying out of sight as the demon strode with purpose. He walked around a large hill, and she followed him.

She jerked to a halt when she found him waiting for her, his machete gripped in his hands.

"Why are you following me?"

"I want to talk."

He scowled. "That's what everyone wants to do. Talk. Useless. We're done talking."

She tightened her hand around her staff. "Who's we?"

His eyes darted over her shoulder for a split second. She spun around, swinging out with her staff and connecting with a blue and black Majock behind her who grunted, bending over for a second. Naya brought the staff up and pushed it backwards like a spear, hard. The heavy clank let her know she had connected with the Lagfel's machete.

She moved sideways to get both of the demons in her line of sight as they advanced on her. "Don't do this. If you continue, you will ruin the realm demons' chance to go to earth."

"Maybe we don't want to go to earth," the Lagfel said.

Energy shot up her back, and she stumbled forward, clumsily trying to turn, even though her muscles protested. She saw the flash of an orange face—Kelmar—before another energy burst took her to her knees. She had never felt such power before. Didn't know it existed in the realm. She pitched forward, catching herself with her hands before landing face-first on the path.

Energy still bubbled under her skin, burning her like a thousand pinpricks. Her eyes closed as she escaped the pain.

CHAPTER 24

Aleksei shook the clan leader's hand, promising to return with the proof needed to convince them. He turned to go, and then frowned when he only saw Marrick. A scowling Marrick. He walked toward him as fast as he could without creating suspicion.

"Where's Naya?"

"Come with me," Marrick said softly.

They walked a few yards away from the dispersing crowd. "What's wrong?" Aleksei asked.

"Naya saw the Lagfel who attacked your compound. She followed him."

"Damn it! Why didn't you go with her?"

"One of us had to stay with you. I told her to let me follow."

"But she said no, of course."

"She was supposed to report in every thirty minutes."

Aleksei's heart clenched. "How late is she?"

"She reported in once, and it's been over forty-five minutes since I heard from her. I can't get her to respond."

He tightened his fists to stop smoke from erupting from his fingertips. "Did she tell you where they were going?"

"She was following them into the foothills."

"Let's go."

As soon as they left the village, they broke into a jog. But after a few minutes, Aleksei jerked to a stop. "Wait. Naya told me the portal devices were interconnected. Can't you link to Naya and track her?"

Marrick hesitated. "I tried."

"And?"

"I can't find her."

"What does that mean? Are you telling me she's dead?" Aleksei's voice rose.

"No. They could be blocking the signal."

"How?"

"The only place in the realm where we can't sense each other are the crystal caves."

"Naya told me about them."

"It's where the Kelmar live," Marrick said.

"So you think they're behind all this?"

"It's looking that way."

Aleksei gazed across the field. "How far are the caves from here?"

"Not far at all."

"Then what are we waiting for?" Aleksei asked.

Marrick nodded. "You're a warrior at heart."

They started to jog again, and Aleksei concentrated on his breathing and pace, as he did on the treadmill every morning. When his breathing hitched, it had nothing to do with the exercise. Naya had to be okay. There were no other acceptable outcomes. Period.

Voices came to Naya first in the darkness. Voices she didn't recognize, but from the tone she could tell they were angry.

"Why did you bring her here? They will come for her now."

"Which is what we want. We now have a bargaining chip for Joran."

Naya took stock of her body, concentrating to see if she had any injuries. For the most part she felt fine, with the exception of having her hands tied. She slowly wiggled her fingers to try and loosen the vines tied around her wrists, but she couldn't get them to budge.

A voice sounded above her. "I know you are awake."

Naya opened her eyes. Saboll, the Kelmar clan leader, stared down as her. Naya attempted to sit up, even though her hands were tied behind her back. Was he behind the protestors?

"Why are you doing this? You have a chance at leaving the realm and going to earth."

"You forget that we have clan members who have gone to earth. The Abstatholm tell us the truth of what earth is really like. Joran left here a month ago to avenge Markal's death and now he is being held hostage.

"He isn't a hostage. He is being held because he broke the law."

"Earth laws."

"Not just earth laws. He attacked a compound with women and children. Which would not be tolerated in the realm either."

"How do you know this?"

"I was there when he"—she nodded toward the demons—"and those two attacked."

"She lies," the Majock said.

"I will hear the truth from Joran. I will claim family rite."

Naya shook her head. "The authorities on earth will not trade him for me."

"She's right," a voice called out. "But they might bargain for me instead."

Naya's stomach dropped as Aleksei appeared in the fire-light. Demons with spears ordered him to halt. What was he doing?

Saboll stood. "So, the famous earther has come to speak to us."

"You wasted a lot of effort to get me here, because I was already planning to visit you anyway."

"We don't need a *visit* from you. We've heard of the lies you spread to the other clans. We will not be as gullible."

"I've already had this conversation with the Lagfel clan leader when he questioned my honesty. I am not here to lie. I'm here to prove we're telling the truth."

"And how to you plan to do that?"

"I plan to stay here."

Naya shook her head. "You don't want to keep him, Saboll. It will bring trouble to your clan."

"It is true I have more say, which means I am a bigger bargaining chip for you."

Saboll glanced between them. "Untie her."

The Kelmar demon cut her restraints and she moved her stiff arms to the front to discover both her hands were asleep. She wanted to wrap her hands around the neck of the demon in front of her, but she couldn't feel her fingers.

"You tell earth that I expect to see Joran in five days' time, or I will declare blood rite," Sabol announced.

She wanted to scream at Aleksei in frustration. *Damn* this stubborn male. He was going to get himself killed.

"Go, Naya," Aleksei said.

"Don't do this."

"Go!"

She left the caves and ran along the cliff until she saw Marrick. Marrick looked behind her and scowled. "He trad-ed himself for you."

She slammed her hands into his chest. "Why did you let him come alone?"

Marrick grabbed her wrists. "Aleksei doesn't want a war. All our progress will be lost if we fight the realm demons."

"You don't think all will be lost if they kill him? They have declared blood rite."

"How much time do we have?"

"Five days."

"I told him it might happen. It's part of his plan."

She jerked her wrists free. "What plan? How to get himself killed?"

"He has five days to convince the Kelmar to work with him. Plus, I can't imagine the other clans are going to be too happy when they hear what has happened."

"We can't rely on them. I'm going to bring the Kelmar back here."

"No. Aleksei said absolutely not."

"He could die."

Marrick grabbed her shoulders. "Listen to me. Aleksei said we couldn't risk letting the Kelmar go. If he is free, he might go after the twins again."

Naya closed her eyes and took a breath to steady her heartbeat. "I can't stand by and let him die, Marrick."

"You assume he would be defeated in the challenge."

"If he goes up against the Kelmar who attacked me, he won't survive. I have never felt that level of power before. I don't know where he is getting it." She paced for a moment. "If we can't attack, then we need to show the other clans that Aleksei means business. That what he has promised so far will happen. You stay here and watch over Aleksei. I'm going to earth to get help."

Fifteen minutes later, Naya ran along a dry riverbed and reached for the necklace she kept under her jumpsuit. *Kyle, are you there?*

Naya? How are things going?

I need you to gather everyone together. We have a situation.

What's happened?

I'll explain everything when I get there. How fast can you get to the compound?

The team is already at the compound. We're having dinner with Misha and Callie. I'll get Boris and Irina to meet us in the conference room.

Naya ran for another half hour, until she was far enough away from the Kelmar to safely open a gate. With the time difference, only a few minutes would have passed on earth. She might make it to the compound before the team made it to the conference room.

Naya opened the portal and stepped through, wishing the portal could wipe away her fears for Aleksei, but that was a fantasy.

She landed in the conference room as the BSR team—Kyle, Jean Luc, Misha, Jason, Talia, and Sabrina—rushed into the room. Even Callie and Kyle's mate, Dalton, were there. Moments later, Boris and Irina hurried in as well.

"What's happened?" Misha asked.

"The Kelmar have taken Aleksei hostage. They want Joran, their clan member, to be returned to them, or they will declare blood rite."

"What's that?" Kyle asked.

"The Kelmar have declared the right to fight for a family member. If he is not returned, they will challenge Aleksei to a fight to the death."

"If we let him go free, can we stop him from coming to earth again?" Callie asked.

Misha put his arm around Callie and pulled her close.

Naya choked out the words. "Aleksei said we should not free the Kelmar. He won't risk the twins' safety."

Callie held her hand over her mouth as a tear ran down her cheek.

"Aleksei has been meeting with the clan leaders, and has promised proof that earth is safe. Callie, I need you and Doyle to contact the original five from the first relocation and get them here quickly. And we also need to see if we can get some of the demons who were enslaved by the demon trafficking as well. Have them ready to travel back to the realm when I reach out to Kyle. We need to prove to the clans that they're okay and being treated well.

"I also need you to gather some clothing together—jackets, jeans, shoes, shirts, in different sizes. Is it something you can collect immediately?"

"Yes," Boris said. "I will send a text out to the compound and have everyone bring clothing to the community center in the next hour."

Naya sighed her relief. "Good. Have them loaded into duffel bags that the original five will take with them to the realm." She looked at the worried faces in front of her. "Aleksei has promised action instead of words, and we will deliver them for him. If we can get the other clans on our side, we may have a chance to stop this without bloodshed. The Kelmar leader has given us five days to return. On earth it equates approximately to a day, which doesn't give us a lot of time."

"Then we even the playing field and go to the realm now," Irina said. The group turned to her. "If we go there now, we'll have the advantage of more time."

Callie cleared her throat. "Doyle, Sylvia, and I will keep the immigration plans going."

"And we will help as needed," Jean Luc said, with the rest of the team agreeing.

"What are we waiting for?" Boris asked. "I'm going back with you to the realm."

Callie and Misha exchanged a glance before Misha spoke. "I'm going too."

"And me," Irina announced.

"Mother—"

"Don't, Boris. I am over a thousand years old, and I can still kick your butt. I'm going."

"I want to come too," Kyle said.

"I don't know if it's a good idea, Kyle," Sabrina said. "We don't know if the realm will make you sick."

Kyle frowned. "What do you mean? I've been to the realm and I was fine."

Sabrina looked between her and Dalton. "We don't know why Joe got so sick in the realm. It could have been his human side, or it could have been because he's part angel. We know some of his angel essence has now passed to you, and it's possible it would make you sick in the realm."

Dalton put his arm around Kyle. "I know you want to be there, but if you do get sick, it will distract them from helping Aleksei."

Kyle growled for a moment. "Fine. I won't go, but I expect Naya to keep us updated on what's going on."

"We will leave in fifteen minutes," Naya announced. "Change into comfortable clothes and shoes made for walking long distances."

Everyone left with the exception of Irina and Kyle, who stood to the side discussing something quietly before Irina dialed her phone. "Sergei, you need to come home. Aleksei is in grave danger. Call the following number and talk to Kyle. She'll pick you up at the airport and explain everything. Please, Grandson. Your family needs you."

She hung up and showed Kyle her phone. "Save this number so you know who it is if he calls you back."

"If?" Kyle asked.

"Sergei travels the world. He might not be in an area with phone reception right now. If we're lucky, he'll call." Irina turned to Naya. "I'll be right back."

Kyle walked over, sat down, and watched Naya pace around the conference table. Why in the world did Aleksei exchange himself for her? It was illogical. She was expendable. He was not.

"Are you okay?" Kyle asked.

"No, I'm angry. When I agreed to allow Aleksei to come to the realm, he promised he would listen to me. That I would be in charge. Now he's being held hostage, and if anything happens to him, it will be my fault."

"How did he get captured to begin with?"

"He didn't. I was taken, and the fool exchanged himself for me."

"Wow, he has turned into a hero. When I first met him, I didn't know he had it in him."

Naya knew he had it in him. He was too damn honorable and self-sacrificing for his own good.

"I don't know what this family will do if something happens to him," Kyle said.

Naya didn't know what *she* would do if something happened to him, so she would not allow it.

No arguments. End of story.

CHAPTER 25

Aleksei watched the demons gathered around the fire. After Naya left, they tied him to a tree where they could see him, but far enough away from the fire that the cold was setting in. Aleksei thought back to the warm fleece jacket he gave to the Dragan clan leader and wished he hadn't gotten carried away. Hindsight.

At least they had tied his hands in the front. It gave him some maneuverability. A rustle sounded to his right, and he turned slightly. A Kelmar female stood outside the firelight staring at him. She dropped a blanket by him and then jerked away as he reached for it.

"I'm sorry. I didn't mean to scare you. Thank you."

She nodded and scurried away. Aleksei settled on the hard ground and pulled the blanket over him. He wondered what Naya was doing. He was surprised she hadn't stormed the clan village. Hopefully Marrick had talked some sense into her. In the meantime, Aleksei still had time to convince the clan leader to listen. All his previous discussions with the clan leaders had been leading to this. He closed his eyes to get some rest, but he kept imagining Naya stretched out on the bed, just as she'd been the night before. When—not if—he got out of this, he and Naya would be having a talk.

Whatever was growing between them was not a fling. He wasn't sure what it was yet, but he wouldn't let her go when he returned to earth. Aleksei drifted off while making mental lists about what he would need to do to convince her to give them a chance.

The next morning, the female from the night before brought him food and water, setting the wooden tray in front of him so he would have to reach for it.

He smiled. "Thank you for the food. I'm Aleksei. What's your name?"

"Lela."

She had dark bags under her eyes, and her hair hung limply around her face. Something wasn't right. Were the clan members abusing her?

"Have you seen Saboll this morning?"

"My father is out for his morning walk."

Father? He needed to see if Lela could give him some insight.

"I would like to talk to him," Aleksei continued.

"You can talk, but he might not be willing to listen."

"I'm here to help the clan."

She tilted her head and stared at him as if he were a puzzle she was trying to solve. "I thought you were here because you're tied up."

Aleksei chuckled. "Very true. But I think we can find a way to work things out. If your clan doesn't want to come to earth, you don't have to."

She leaned a little closer to him, and lowered her voice. "Most of us don't want to stay here."

"Does your father know?"

"No—"

"What are you two talking about?" One of the Kelmar males demanded.

"Nothing, Tarem."

Tarem marched up and kicked the wooden tray, spilling Aleksei's food on the ground and grabbing Lela's arm. A scream of pain erupted from her.

Aleksei struggled to get to his feet. "Stop! You're hurting her!"

After another moment, the Kelmar let go of Lela, and she collapsed on the ground next to Aleksei. He reached for her with his bound hands, but Tarem held up his hand, light bursting from him and slamming into Aleksei's chest.

Aleksei doubled over from the burning pain shooting through him.

"You don't touch her," Tarem growled, sparks flowing between his fingers.

Lela sat up as if to block Aleksei's body with her own. "You can't kill him. Father is expecting to trade him for Joran."

Tarem closed his fist and the light dissipated. "I'm watching you," he growled before walking away.

"Are you okay?" Aleksei asked. "What did he do to you?"

"Touch hurts me. It drains my energy."

"You're like a conduit for power."

She scrunched her face at his words.

"It means the other demons are able to increase their powers by taking your energy."

"Yes. Which is why Tarem is so powerful. But it doesn't last long, and then he comes back for more."

"But it's making you sick. He's taking too much."

"He doesn't care. It's only about being the strongest. Soon I will have nothing left."

"You mean they'll kill you. Why don't you tell your father?"

She shook her head and stood. "I can't."

"Then I'll tell him."

"No! Tarem will kill you, and if you die, they'll shut the realm off for good, and never let any of us leave."

Aleksei opened his mouth to argue, but she cut him off.

"Please. I can handle this for now. If you ever speak to my father, you need to tell him about the immigration. That is what matters."

Aleksei agreed to calm her down, even though he would step in if he had to. How could a father let his daughter be treated this way?

Naya sat at the small table they had pulled out of her hut and placed in the field so the group could gather around her. Irina sat in the chair next to her, while Boris, Misha, and her portal guards stood.

Naya took the paper and pencil she had brought from earth and started to make a list. Aleksei would be so proud of her.

"Marrick has gone to earth to get the realm demons, along with the clothing they have collected. I will have a portal guard escort each one to their respective clans, with the exception of the Kelmar. We will talk to him about his clan and ask why they are so resistant to earth." She wrote another item. "Hopefully we can get the other clan leaders to stand with us when we speak to the Kelmar."

"What about the Majock clan?" Irina asked. "Aleksei hasn't met with them yet, correct?"

"Correct."

"I'll meet with them," Boris said. "I'll relay Aleksei's message and let the realm demon describe his experiences on earth."

Naya wrote Boris's name next to the item on her checklist. "Good. Today we'll try to convince the other clans to stand with us. Tomorrow we go for Aleksei."

The group nodded in agreement just as one of the guards announced that Marrick was back. Naya watched him approach with eleven other demons. Eleven? She recognized the five realm demons who had been part of the first relocation, so she assumed the other five were the demons who had been part of the demon trafficking, but there was also a tall, blond male walking alongside Marrick.

"Sergei!" Irina jumped up and rushed over to him, throwing her arms around him as he bent down and hugged her.

So this was Aleksei's younger brother. Both Misha and Boris seemed stunned to see him. Misha grabbed him in an awkward hug before Sergei stepped back and nodded to his father.

"How did you find out what happened?" Boris asked.

"I called him," Irina said. "We need our whole family here."

Boris cleared his throat. "Thank you for coming."

Sergei gave him a slight bow.

Naya didn't have time to knock their heads together and tell them to get along. So she went back to the plan. "Let's talk through what will happen when we meet with the Kelmar tomorrow night."

She would make as many checklists as needed, and talk through the steps a million times, if it meant Aleksei's safe return.

CHAPTER 26

Aleksei spent the day trying to have a discussion with the clan leader. But every time he got the demon's attention for a few moments, Tarem or the Lagfel or the Majock demon would interrupt and drag him away to discuss clan business.

Aleksei was running out of time. He had told Naya not to attack, but she was a demon of action. He feared the longer he was held captive, the more likely she would try something to free him. If he had to face the blood rite, he wouldn't lie down without a fight. But he hoped it wouldn't come to that...for all their sakes.

A shout sounded across the village, and clan members came out of their huts and clustered around their leader.

Aleksei stood and attempted to see what drew everyone's attention. His heart clenched—actually clenched. He had never understood the saying until now. Naya strode purposefully toward the clan leader, her staff in hand. Her set expression told him she meant business. She was going to face off with the entire clan.

But she was not alone.

Naya led the way, but behind her was his family! Boris, Misha—even Babushka was here, for Fate's sake. What were they thinking?

When he spotted the male walking next to Babushka, he froze. Sergei. He didn't want to know what they told him to get him home.

Next came the four other clan leaders and the original five demons who relocated to earth. And behind them were other clan members. In a show of solidarity? Leave it to Naya to put his plan into action.

She came to a stop in front of the Kelmar leader and pressed the tip of her staff into the earth. Aleksei watched her hand as she adjusted her grip on the staff.

Saboll stared at her and then looked over the gathering behind her. "Where is Joran?"

"He will not be returned to you. He is facing sentencing for his attacks on earth, as the Majock and Lagfel behind you should be doing as well."

"So you are willingly sacrificing the earther. As the head of my clan, I claim blood rite for the loss of my clansman."

"And as the head of my clan, I claim right of refusal." The voice rang out behind her, as Boris stepped up beside Naya.

"No!" Aleksei shouted. He would not allow his father to fight his battles.

"You are the head of your clan?" Saboll asked.

Boris crossed his arms. "Yes. As head, I can determine who will face you in the rite."

The clan leader's eyes narrowed. "As can I."

Tarem stepped forward, shoulders back, chest out. Of course it would be him. Aleksei would not allow anyone else to fight him. He was too powerful.

Before he could protest, Naya spoke. "Before we start killing each other, I demand to speak in Aleksei's defense. But first, untie him so he can be part of this."

Saboll nodded, and a Kelmar clan member untied him and brought him over to stand on the Kelmar side. He looked over at Naya, and she gazed back for a moment before continuing.

"Aleksei and his family have brought two groups of demons to earth. This is not a lie. The immigrants are doing well on earth. The other clan leaders asked for proof of this claim, and as Aleksei promised to them, we have brought proof in the form of the first five immigrants standing behind me. They came back here willingly to tell the clans about their experiences on earth.

A tall Kelmar demon came to stand next to Naya, and Saboll gaped at him. "Kall? You have returned."

Kall nodded. "I came to tell you that earth is everything the realm is not. Our clans have a chance to thrive on earth. If we kill the demon responsible for helping us, nothing will be the same. Why would the earth demons be willing to trust us after that?"

The Dragan clan leader spoke up. "Listen to him, Saboll. If you don't want to leave the realm, you don't have to, but it doesn't give you the right to destroy the opportunity for others to leave. We have spent a millennium trapped here. Now we have the freedom to choose."

Saboll shook his head. "The Abstatholm—"

"Have lied to you," Naya said. "I don't know why they're spreading these stories. It could be fear. Even though many want to go to earth, the idea of leaving what we know is terrifying.

"Or maybe they want to control the immigration on their terms. Before the official relocations, clan members were sent to earth by the Abstatholm, and we now know they forced those realm demons to work as slaves for them, threatening their families in the realm if they did not obey.

"Now that demons are able to go to earth without their help, it has taken away their ability to control and manipulate."

Aleksei was floored. Naya was amazing. He knew she was a good leader of the guard, but this...this was way beyond simply being a good leader. She was a diplomat and a soldier in one powerful package.

Naya continued. "I have brought back several of those who were promised a better life by the Abstatholm, who will tell you what happened to them. It was the earthers who freed them from their slavery. Not the other way around."

The Lagfel and Majock standing behind Saboll ran toward Naya. Before Aleksei could react, his Babushka took charge.

"No!" Irina said, flicking her wrist and lifting the two demons off the ground, leaving them to dangle in the air, their legs kicking like children throwing a tantrum.

Instead of running toward Naya, the Kelmar demon Tarem launched himself at Lela, who was standing off to the side.

"Don't touch her!" Aleksei yelled before tackling the Kelmar.

Then he convulsed for what seemed an endless time while energy blasted through him.

Misha shouted, and the Kelmar shot up into the air, and then hit the ground, hard. Boris ran over, and when Tarem started to get up, slammed a fist into his face. The demon flopped over, unconscious. *Way to go, Dad.*

"What is the meaning of this?" Saboll bellowed.

Aleksei struggled to sit up. A hand reached out to him, and he looked up to find Sergei standing over him. He grabbed his younger brother's hand and stood on shaky legs.

"He has been draining Lela of her power. He's killing her," Aleksei replied.

Saboll turned to her. "Why didn't you tell me?"

"He threatened you, Father. Said he would kill you and take over the clan if I told you the truth."

He reached for her, and she flinched. "Oh, my child. I should be the one to protect you, not the other way around. I have failed you." He looked around at the gathered crowd. "I have failed all of you. I have let my own fear cloud my judgement. It was much easier to believe what my clan members were telling me than risk sending us to a new world." Saboll blew out a harsh breath. "What do we do now?"

Aleksei looked over at Naya.

She nodded at him before responding. "Now we sit down and discuss next steps."

They had been talking for an hour, and the clan leaders wanted to discuss things apart from the others for a moment.

Aleksei was finally able to take a breath, but when he looked over at his family, he had a hard time swallowing around the lump in his throat. His family had come for him. They stood behind him when he needed them most. He wasn't surprised...well, if he was being honest with himself, he was surprised to see Sergei. How in the world had they tracked him down and gotten him here? But he was here.

And Naya. The lump in his throat grew. She was the impetus behind all of this. If not for her... He didn't want to think about the alternative. What he wanted to do was pull her into his arms. He watched her walk toward him, so powerful, so beautiful.

"I have so much to say to you," he said.

Her eyes tightened on him. "And I you, but now is not the time."

He nodded. "You're right. I want you to reach out to Kyle and tell her we need Sabrina to come to the realm. I want her to examine Lela and see if she can help her. Then I want her to see if she can help set up an infirmary in the realm. They need more than clothes and food here."

"I'll speak to her now."

Naya started to walk away, and Aleksei placed his hand on her arm to stop her. "Thank you."

Naya smiled slightly before walking away.

Aleksei watched the crowd around him. He wasn't surprised to see Irina, Boris, and Misha in the middle of the group talking to the realm demons. Sergei stood off to the side, watching the demons around him. Aleksei approached and stood next to him.

"It's good to see you again, brother. Thank you for coming."

Sergei turned to him. "I'm glad you're okay. I didn't know what to expect here."

"It's a lot to take in, and you got thrown into the deep end without any preparation."

"If Naya's plan hadn't worked, I'm not sure what I could've done to help."

Aleksei sighed and glanced away from his brother for a moment to squelch his frustration. When would his brother realize powers or lack of them did not define him? He caught sight of Lela, standing apart from the rest of the demons. Her father had tried to get her to go back to her hut, but she had refused. "I actually think you *can* help. I want you to meet Lela."

Sergei followed his gaze. "The Kelmar female? She's terrified. Why do you think meeting a strange male would be helpful right now?"

"She needs to know not everyone will try to steal her powers. She needs a protector from the rest of the demons who will be surrounding her for the next few days."

"And how can I keep her safe? I wouldn't be able to stop anyone from touching her."

"You don't give yourself enough credit. I think she needs to feel safe with one person who can't steal from her."

Sergei's face fell. "Because I'm a null."

Aleksei hated when his brother called himself that. "Sergei, you have always said your lack of powers is a disadvantage, but now, in this instance, it is exactly what is needed to help a female who has been abused. Are you willing to help her for a few days? And are you okay with me telling her about you?"

His brother hesitated before answering. "Yes."

Aleksei threw his arm around his brother's shoulder, surprising him. "Excellent. Let me check with her first."

He walked over to Lela, and she actually smiled slightly as he approached.

"Lela, how are you feeling?"

"Better. Thank you for protecting me earlier."

"Of course." She still looked exhausted, so he decided to broach the possibility of Sabrina's visit with her later. Now he wanted to see if she was okay with having Sergei sit with her.

He looked around at the crowd. "I'm hoping these conversations will help the immigrations move more quickly and smoothly."

"I'm just happy my father is seeing reason now."

"Your father is unsure of the future. Fear is a powerful motivator."

Her smile dimmed. "I know."

"My family is here to learn as well." He started to point them out. "That is my father, Boris."

"You look like him except for your eyes."

"Yes. And that is my grandmother, Irina."

"She is an amazing warrior. Was she going to stand up for you during the rite?"

"If she had her way, yes. Although my father would have had something to say about that. The male standing next to her is my brother, Misha and over there is my younger brother, Sergei."

Aleksei continued. "I'd like to introduce you to him if you're willing. He knows nothing about the realm, and I wonder if he could sit here with you so you can explain things to him."

"I...why me?"

"Because he's standing over there by himself and you are sitting by yourself." Aleksei knelt down to be eye-level with her. "Sergei feels like he is an outsider most of the time. If I tell you something about him, can I trust you to keep his secret?"

She nodded.

"Sergei has never developed powers. So seeing this world is a bit overwhelming to him. I thought it would be good to let you sit with him. And I also thought it would be nice for you to spend time with someone who won't try to steal your powers."

Her eyes widened as she looked over at Sergei. "Really? He can't hurt me?"

Aleksei's heart ached at her question. "He can't. You have my word."

"I would like to meet him."

Aleksei grinned and beckoned to Sergei. "Wonderful."

Sergei arrived a minute later and sat down so he wasn't towering over Lela.

"Lela, this is Sergei. As you can see, I got both the looks and the brains in the family."

Lela chuckled. "And modesty."

Aleksei laughed. "Exactly!" He looked at his brother. "At the rate things are going with the clan discussions, I think we might be at it for a couple days. And so you two aren't bored while we're talking politics, I thought Lela could tell you about the realm, and you can tell her about earth." He turned to look at Lela. "Sergei has traveled all over earth. He will have plenty of stories to tell you."

Lela looked at Sergei and swallowed before dropping her eyes to the ground. Sergei looked like he had eaten something rotten. Holy Fates, it was like a junior high dance. Aleksei hoped the two of them would have something to say to each other instead of staring at the ground.

But then, since he and Naya learned they could get along, he believed in miracles.

CHAPTER 27

Naya looked around at all the tired faces.

They had spent the past few days meeting with the clan leaders and various clan members to plan for the future. Not just the future of those who came to earth, but also for those who chose to remain in the realm.

Now Aleksei and his family were returning to earth. One of the first things Aleksei did after the Kelmar let him go was to have Sabrina come to the realm to check on Lela and other demons who had health issues. Sabrina decided to stay longer so she could help with medical issues and establish a better infirmary in the realm.

Handshakes were exchanged, and backs were slapped as the Chesnokovs and the portal guard said goodbye. Naya's heart felt hollow. She and Aleksei had not been able to spend any time alone together.

Aleksei walked over to her and smiled. "I understand from Marrick that you really were the driving force behind bringing the clans together and having them face the Kelmar."

"I didn't do anything you wouldn't have done yourself. We've made great strides these past days."

"I agree. And now I need to get back and work on next steps."

She looked away from him for a second. Was he trying to tell her goodbye? That their time together was over?

"Can you come to earth for a few days?" He took a step closer. "I could use your help."

"I'll have to talk to Marrick—"

"I already spoke to him. He thinks it's a good idea for you to come with me."

Naya felt her eyebrows rise. "Oh, does he?"

"He said you shouldn't forget your notebook. That you have been keeping notes and a checklist." A wicked grin broke out on Aleksei's face.

She was so going to make her second-in-charge pay. "Fine. I'll come and get things set up the right way."

Aleksei barked out a laugh. Out of the corner of her eye, Naya caught Irina watching them.

"It's time to take you all home," Naya announced.

Marrick walked over and handed her the notebook.

"We will be having words when I get back," she said with a fake glare.

Marrick winked at her, and her mouth fell open. He had been spending way too much time with Aleksei and his brothers. Naya opened the portal. Light coalesced until it was the size of a large door.

Naya led the group through the portal, and moments later she arrived in the Shamat community center. The BSR team, including Kyle, Jean-Luc, Talia, and Jason, were waiting for them, along with Callie and the twins.

When Misha walked through the portal, Callie and the twins launched themselves at him. He pulled them into his arms, and the boys started peppering him with questions about the realm until Callie shushed them.

Kyle grinned. "Thank God you're all home."

"Where's Sabrina?" Jason asked.

"Sabrina has decided to stay awhile longer to check on the health of some of the clan members, and to figure out a way to set up better medical care in the realm," Aleksei said.

Jason frowned. "You left her there alone?"

"Several of my portal guard are watching over her, Jason," Naya said.

Jason's frown tightened.

"She'll be safe," Naya said, trying to reassure him.

Kyle clapped her hands together. "So tell us what happened when you confronted the Kelmar. Naya only gave me bits and pieces of the story. I want the full details."

The family took turns telling the story.

"So if you hadn't convinced the clan leader, Aleksei would have fought the badass Kelmar demon," Kyle said.

Boris shook his head. "I would have chosen someone from the family to fight."

"It would have been me," Irina said.

"*Mother.*"

"*Son.* I am still the most powerful, although I think Mikhail could give me a run for my money." She winked at Misha.

Aleksei stepped between them. "It's a good thing we don't have to worry about who would be the challenger."

"Very true. I don't know about the rest of you, but I need a shower, something decadent to eat, and my bed," Irina announced.

Naya watched the crowd disperse except for Kyle and Aleksei.

Aleksei leaned closer to Naya. "I'm going to drop off our notebooks in the office and then I'll be back in a few minutes."

Naya nodded and started to pace as she thought about what could have gone wrong.

"I knew you could do it. You kept everyone safe," Kyle said as she took a seat at the table.

"If it wasn't for me, they would have never had to go there in the first place."

"And if you had not gone there, we wouldn't be in the position we are now. I'm sorry Aleksei was taken hostage, but it brought everything to a head, and now the clans want to work with us."

"I still should have been more careful."

"Why are you still beating yourself up about this? You saved him." After a moment, Kyle gaped at her. "Holy crap. You like Aleksei."

Naya stopped pacing. "This isn't about me liking him. It's about me failing to protect him."

Kyle chuckled. "Oh. My. God. You slept with him." She leaned forward. "Is he good in bed? No! Don't answer that."

Naya jerked around toward the door to make sure no one had returned. "Now is not the time—"

"Now is exactly the time. I thought you guys weren't getting along. You told me he was infuriating and egotistical."

"I was mistaken."

"What happened to change your mind?"

"He is an honorable male. Look at everything he's done so far to arrange the immigration. He was willing to come to the realm, and he almost ended up sacrificing himself to save me."

"He does grow on you. When I first met him. I wanted to wipe the arrogant smirk off his face. Now I can't imagine anyone else running the immigration bureau. So where do you go from here?"

"There is nowhere to go. Aleksei is not looking for a relationship. He is dedicated to his job, and once the realm demons have been brought to earth, he will prepare for his future job as clan leader by finding an appropriate mate."

"Aleksei said that to you?"

"Yes. Before we left to go to the realm."

"Which was before you two knocked boots."

"I don't wear boots. I don't know what you're referring to."

"It means you two had sex. Things have changed for you now, for both of you."

"There's still a lot to do with the immigration."

"So you do it together."

Could it be as simple as that? Could she continue to work with him, hoping it turned into something more? Because if she was honest with herself, it had been something more for her from the beginning.

Before Naya could respond, Aleksei came back into the room. Kyle got up and walked over to him while Naya held her breath, wondering what Kyle was about to say.

"You did a great job, Aleksei. I'm so glad you're heading up the immigration bureau." Kyle held out her hand, and Aleksei shook it.

"Aw, what the hell." Kyle pulled him in for a quick hug. "Way to go, brother of mine. You two get some rest. You both deserve it."

Kyle winked at Naya before she left.

"What now?" Naya asked.

Aleksei smiled, his eyes twinkling at her. "I like Babushka's plan. Shower. Something decadent to eat. And bed." He held out his hand. "Unless you have something else in mind?"

"No. It sounds just right."

They walked together, almost touching, out of the room and down the hall until they reached the outside door. Once outside, they crossed the grass and walked down the street until they reached a house made out of large, tan stones and blue-painted wood. He took her hand and led her into the house, then pulled her down the hall into a bedroom with dark furniture and the biggest bed she had ever seen.

Aleksei opened a door that led into a bathroom and turned on the shower. Then he came back out with a grin.

"What are you smiling about?" Naya asked.

He pulled his shirt off. "I can't wait to get in the shower."

She nodded. "I'm sure it will be nice to clean up after your captivity."

He pushed down his pants. "Why aren't you getting undressed?"

"I thought I would wait until you're finished so I can then take a shower as well."

Aleksei stalked over to her in his boxers. "We can shower together."

The idea more than intrigued her. "We don't have showers in the realm. The first shower I took was when I stayed with Irina. I don't know what the rules are."

He pulled her armor off. "There are no rules, Naya. Since you've only recently experienced a shower, I would be happy to educate you in the niceties of shower sex."

"How very generous of you."

"I think so," Aleksei said as he opened the fasteners on her jumpsuit and pushed it off her shoulders, letting it hit the floor. His eyes warmed as he looked her up and down. "You are glorious."

She raised her eyebrow at him. "You are overdressed."

Aleksei laughed. "No problem."

He pushed the boxers off his hips, and she sucked in a breath at his beauty. Aleksei leaned forward and brushed his lips against hers before holding out his hand to her. She grasped it, and he pulled her into the bathroom and then into the large shower.

Warm water cascaded over her as Aleksei reached for the soap and began to bathe her. She had trouble not squirming under his ministrations as his talented hands cleansed her thoroughly.

Then she returned the favor.

And then her generous lover taught her about sex in the shower and several other areas of the house. He was a great teacher, and she a ready student. Now they lay intertwined, panting and sweaty.

Aleksei chuckled, the sound vibrating through her.

She propped her chin on his chest to look at him. "What?"

"I think we're going to need another shower."

She laid her head on his chest and laughed with him. After a few moments, he placed his fingers under her chin so she looked up at him again.

"Glorious," he whispered, and kissed her lightly before picking her up.

She had never been carried before, and she tensed in his arms.

He stopped. "It's okay to let someone take care of you, Naya. Let me carry you."

She rested her head against his chest and listened to his heartbeat speed up as he carried her through the house and into the bathroom again.

CHAPTER 28

Naya woke up as the sun came through the windows. Warmth ran along her back. She looked over her shoulder to see Aleksei sleeping against her. She shouldn't get used to watching him sleep, but he was unguarded then. She ran her fingers over his eyebrows and down his cheek before rubbing them lightly over his lips. After a moment, he nipped at her fingers and she gasped.

His eyes opened. Beautiful green eyes full of mischief. "Are you having fun?"

"Possibly."

He kissed her pointer finger before pulling her closer to him. "Good."

"We should get up, Aleksei."

"I would love to stay in bed with you all day, but I agree. There's a lot to be done. You're going to stay for a while, yes?"

Naya smiled at the question. He sounded like his father and Misha. "Yes. I'm going to go to Irina's. I left the clothes Kyle bought me there, and I would like to not wear my realm clothes."

"I would like you to not wear clothes too."

She clucked her tongue at him. "I can't walk around naked, Aleksei, so you will have to compromise and let me wear earth clothes."

"You have turned into a diplomat, for sure."

They climbed out of bed and got dressed before Aleksei went to his office. At this point in the day, Irina would be at the community kitchen serving the guards.

Naya walked to Irina's and opened the back kitchen door, which Irina left unlocked during the day. As she headed toward the hall leading to the bedrooms, she heard voices in the living room. She stepped around the kitchen table to let Irina know she was in the house, but the subject of the conversation stopped her.

She peeked around the wall to see several elders in a heated discussion with Irina.

"Even if we do agree to let Aleksei rule now that we know Misha has the stronger powers, he has shown interest in the portal guard," one of the older males stated.

"So what?" Irina demanded.

"Irina, you know that, due to conflict of interest, you won't be able to vote in this matter," the female next to her said.

"I'm well aware of that. However, it doesn't mean I can't voice my opinion. Are you saying you wouldn't let him be clan leader if he was mated to Naya? We don't even know if Naya and Aleksei will be able to have children together."

"But we don't know if they can't, so it's still an issue."

"What about Misha?" Irina said. "He is with a human now."

"Misha's children will be part human and part Shamat," the male said.

"Naya is half Shamat!"

"And she is also half Pavel. The Pavels have alienated practically all the clans on earth. One of Aleksei's children will be the future leader of this clan. What do you think the clan's reaction will be if the child takes after the Pavel?"

"I think now the realm demons are coming to earth that everything is going to change for us. We have to be willing to accept that the clans are not going to remain the same."

"It may be true, Irina, but I am not sure our clan should be the guinea pig for change."

Naya backed up against the wall and closed her eyes while they continued to discuss her future. After she pulled herself back together, she walked quietly out the back door and down the street, away from Irina's, and away from the community center. She kept walking around the compound, looking at the wonderful community Aleksei's clan had built.

She would not be the reason Aleksei wasn't allowed to rule. It would destroy him. He was an amazing leader, and he was going to combine the two demon worlds into one if it killed him. And when Boris finally decided to step down, Aleksei would lead the clan with a passion surpassing every other leader.

No, she could not stay with him. And even if she did, what would be the point? Aleksei had a fifty-year plan. He would settle down with a Shamat demon at the right time, and have the kind of children who would appease the elders.

It was time to put a plan in place. She could do this. She had learned from the best.

Several hours later, she wasn't surprised when Aleksei found her sitting on a bench by the lake next to the community center.

"There you are. I've been wondering where you were hiding." He looked at her jumpsuit. "I thought you were going to change into some earth clothes?"

She shook her head and gazed out at the lake for a few more moments, needing to fortify herself for what she was about to say.

He walked in front of her, blocking the view, and she allowed herself to meet his concerned eyes.

"Is something wrong?"

"I can't do this."

"Do what, exactly?"

She closed her eyes, not sure if her declaration was that she couldn't be with him, or she couldn't leave him. "I can't stay here. I can't be what you want me to be."

"And what do you think I want you to be?" he asked in a soft voice.

She opened her eyes. "You need someone beside you who will be able to help you run this clan. A negotiator. Someone who knows the right thing to say at the right time."

"You know the right words, Naya. If it weren't for you, I wouldn't be here right now. You are just as responsible for saving the realm demons as I, maybe more so."

"You are destined to rule this clan, Aleksei. I don't want that. My life has been all about duty, honor, and responsibility. Once the rest of the realm demons are brought to earth, I will be free to be who I want to be."

His eyes tightened at the corners. "And who do you want to be?"

"I don't know the answer. I have a whole new world to discover, and then I can make a decision. I don't want to be locked down."

"Have I done something to upset you?"

Naya shook her head quickly. "No, not at all. You told me I should be planning for my future, and I am taking your advice to heart. After what happened in the realm, and knowing what you will be faced with every day, running the bureau and eventually your clan, I know I don't want that kind of life."

Naya rushed on. "Besides, you were the one who told me you couldn't promise a future between us. It makes sense to break things off now. We had an adventure together. Now we spend the next few years bringing the realm demons to earth, and after we can both follow our dreams. They just happen to be in opposite directions."

Aleksei's jaw muscles tightened as he stared at her, hard—as if he wanted to reach into her mind and read her thoughts. She returned his stare, holding her gaze steady and praying she didn't give herself away. She stood.

"I'm going to go back to the realm. There is much to do there as well."

He backed up a step, and she stopped herself from reaching for him.

He finally gave a sharp nod. "I understand."

He understood? How could he understand when she understood nothing anymore?

CHAPTER 29

Three days after Naya left, Aleksei was still having a hard time managing to take a full breath. He felt like someone had hit him in the chest with a fireball.

And he hadn't heard from her. Days of pain for him would equate to weeks in the realm for her, but he had heard nothing. Even Kyle said she was being exceptionally quiet. What had he done? Had he pushed too hard? He knew they were different, that she felt confined by his need to plan, but was that enough to throw away what they had together?

But what did they have together? He couldn't quantify it. He was used to charts and lists and timelines, but feelings were foreign to him. And relationships were not only foreign, but otherworldly. And he didn't miss the irony in that thought.

He got up from his desk and wandered out to the main office. Callie was typing away on her laptop until Aleksei stopped beside her.

"Yes, Aleksei?"

"Did I hear you tell Doyle earlier that Kyle is coming over tonight for dinner?"

"Yes. Now that Misha is spending so much time here, I also get to spend time with his teammates as well."

"And you're okay with that?"

Callie blushed. "Of course. I didn't mean it the way it sounded. I actually love spending time with them."

"I want to talk to Kyle if she has a couple of minutes."

"I'll let her know. She can run down to your house while Misha grills our dinner."

"Actually, I'll be here. Can you have her stop by the office?"

"Sure." Callie frowned slightly. "You have been working day and night here for the past few days, Aleksei. Is everything okay? I can help with some more of the plans, or we can see about hiring some more help if you're that swamped."

He shook his head. "I'm fine. I'm playing a little catch-up after being in the realm. Nothing to worry about."

For a moment she looked like she was going to protest, but finally nodded and went back to work. Once back in his office, he shut the door. He had been spending a lot of time here, but work was the only thing keeping his mind sufficiently occupied right now.

If his new plan came together, he would be able to take a breath again.

A knock at his office door brought Aleksei out of his musings. He looked at the clock and realized it had been over an hour since he spoke to Callie. He called out, and the door opened. Kyle sauntered into the office with her mate, Joe, behind her. He should have known Joe would be coming to dinner as well.

"Hey, Aleksei. What's up?" Kyle said.

"Thanks for stopping by. Both of you. I need a favor."

Kyle walked over to his desk and picked up a paperweight. "Name it."

"Can I borrow your realm crystal for a few minutes?"

Kyle set the weight down and cocked her head to look at him. The gesture reminded him of Naya, and the pain in his chest intensified.

"It's not something I can relay to Naya?"

He should have known she wouldn't be easy to convince. "No."

"We don't even know if it will work between the two of you," she countered.

And hadn't she just hit the nail on the head? "I need to try, Kyle." He swallowed. "Please."

He waited for her to fight him. Instead she reached under her shirt and pulled out the necklace with the red crystal, undid the clasp, and handed it to him.

"If I can help, you'll let me know?" she asked.

He nodded at her while Joe watched them both with a bit of confusion.

"I'll come get it after dinner," she said.

Joe held out his hand, and Kyle took it, as they left the room.

Aleksei took a deep breath and sat down at his desk. He wrapped his hand around the crystal, letting it heat in his palm. Closing his eyes, he reached out to her with his mind.

Naya.

Nothing.

Naya, can you hear me?

Yes, Aleksei. Why are you reaching out to me? Has something happened to Kyle?

No, she's fine. I asked her to lend me the crystal so I can talk to you. His mind went blank. Words were his friends...until they weren't anymore. *I miss you, Naya. I don't understand why we can't see where we can go with this. We'll be handling the immigration for several more years, and will be working side by side, and my father won't be stepping down any time soon. I don't want to force you into being my mate, or make you feel like I'm trapping you.*

Aleksei—

Can't we spend time together?

Silence.

Aleksei held his breath.

I have made my decision. You have taught me to want something different from the life I am leading now.

Naya. Let's get together and talk some more.

He actually felt her sigh in his head. *I didn't want to tell you this, but Marrick and I have come to an understanding.*

An understanding? Even though they were using telepathy, Aleksei choked on the words.

When we have finished with the immigration, we're going to see the world together.

Anger bubbled under his skin like lava. *Were you involved with him when we were together?*

No. We are teammates and best friends. I want to see if it can evolve into something more, as does he.

Aleksei closed his eyes. *Very well. We have called an immigration meeting tomorrow. We need to discuss several things about the new plans to supply items to the realm on a regular basis. I...the team needs you there.*

She hesitated before replying. *Of course.*

Goodbye, Naya. Aleksei dropped the crystal on his desk before he could hear another word from her.

He didn't feel bad for lying about a fictitious meeting if it got her here. She wanted to cut ties and tell him she now had an understanding with Marrick? Then she could damn well do it to his face.

The next morning Aleksei paced back and forth in the community center's meeting room, his shoes echoing in the empty space.

The wall started to move, and Aleksei's heart sped up as the portal opened. And then Marrick walked through. Alone.

"Where is Naya?" Aleksei demanded.

Marrick looked around the empty space. "She asked me to be the liaison for earth."

The words gutted him. She wasn't even going to see him anymore? What kind of crap was she pulling?

Aleksei crossed his arms to stop himself from wrapping his hands around the demon's neck. "She didn't bother to tell me."

Marrick stared at him. "There is a lot going on right now with the clans, and the doctor traveling around the realm."

He narrowed his eyes on the large demon. "I'm well aware of that. I need you to clarify something for me. Apparently Naya no longer wants to see me. She told me you have an understanding. That you plan to travel the world together once the demon relocations are complete. Is that true?"

Marrick's eyes flared for a moment. "Yes."

Aleksei froze for a moment, then managed to breathe. "I think you're lying. Why would you have let me be with her if you want to be with her?"

"Because I want her to be happy."

"You love her," Aleksei blurted.

Marrick nodded.

"And you don't think I can make her happy."

Marrick hesitated. "It doesn't matter what I think. It matters what she thinks."

Aleksei backed up a step, locking his knees to keep himself upright. "Go back to the realm. Tell her I won't bother her anymore. But I still need the guard's help with the immigration."

"Of course. We will see it through."

The portal opened and Marrick disappeared through the flowing energy. Aleksei watched as the light faded away. He wanted to leave, but his legs wouldn't cooperate. He wasn't sure how long he stared at the wall before his legs actually decided to work again. He didn't know when he would be able to say the same about his heart.

———◄○►———

Marrick opened the door to her hut without knocking and slammed it shut.

"What have you done, Naya?"

He was angry. Marrick was usually even-tempered, but his tense body and narrowed eyes told her he was furious.

She opened her mouth and then closed it again.

"You told Aleksei we are together now?"

"No—"

"You told him we have an understanding. What's he supposed to think?"

"That I don't want to be with him anymore!"

"But you haven't told me why. You came back from earth weeks ago, and the light has gone out of your eyes. Did he hurt you?"

"No. He didn't do anything to me."

"Then why?"

Naya clenched her fists. "I overheard the Shamat elders talking about refusing Aleksei as clan leader if he mated me. That any children we have would be part Pavel and not fit to rule the clan."

Marrick scowled. "And Aleksei didn't say anything?"

"He wasn't there."

"You don't think he would stand up for you?"

"I think he would."

"Then what is the problem?" Marrick growled.

"The problem is he would lose the very thing he has spent his whole life preparing for!"

She shot to her feet, and the world spun. Marrick yelled her name, but his voice sounded far away as the world kept spinning until she closed her eyes and let go.

Naya sighed as Sabrina looked her over again. She was fine. She had gotten dizzy. She hadn't even fainted, really. She opened her eyes moments after Marrick had carried her to her bed. Now Sabrina refused to let her get up until she was finished with her examination.

"You shouldn't be spending time with me when there are others who might need your help," Naya grumbled.

"I think they will survive for a few moments." She sat back with a grin. "You're not sick."

"I could have told you that."

"I think you're pregnant."

Naya blinked. "What? Impossible."

"I actually think it's very possible."

"I'm not a fool, Sabrina. I would have known if I was having my cycle. He would have known as well."

Sabrina pursed her lips. "You didn't start portal jumping until recently, correct?"

"All the guards can jump between the in-between and the realm, but Marrick and I were given the ability to jump to earth about a year ago."

"And every time you jump, your body goes through a massive time change. Hours become days and vice versa. That could wreak havoc on a female's system."

She couldn't be pregnant with Aleksei's baby. But Sabrina's face told her she was.

Sabrina sat down across from her. "I know it's a lot to take in. Do you think you'll come to earth to have the baby?"

"I don't see why I need to. Females have been having babies in the realm for a millennia."

"True. But the baby's father is on earth."

Naya shook her head.

"I'm a Succubus, I can sense sexual tension a mile away. Whenever you and Aleksei are within ten feet of each other, the room heats up."

"We're no longer together. It's not serious."

"For whom?"

Naya's heart pinched in his chest. "Please do not say anything to him."

Sabrina frowned. "I won't. Doctors swear an oath. I can't tell him about your health if you tell me not to."

A baby. Could it be true?

She couldn't tell Aleksei.

He was destined to lead, and she would not be the person to destroy his dreams. When he spoke to her telepathically, he hadn't actually said he wanted to be with her forever. He had his fifty-year plan. How would a one-quarter Pavel baby fit into that? She couldn't force Aleksei to choose between his calling and a baby he hadn't planned for with a female he wasn't planning to mate.

CHAPTER 30

Aleksei pounded the treadmill. He had passed his normal ten-mile run several miles ago, but he couldn't get himself to stop, even with his lungs burning. The rhythm kept him sane for the small amount of time he could escape and not think about...things.

He stumbled slightly and righted himself, hitting the button to slow down. He didn't need to shoot off the back of the damn treadmill. He slowed to a jog and then a walk before the machine turned off. He attempted to wipe his face with a towel, but he could do nothing for the soaking wet clothes clinging to him. He nearly staggered over to the long hall and formed a fireball on his palm. He threw it, and it hit the target. Then he formed another ball, and another, letting them rip away as fast as he could form them.

Fireball after fireball shot from his fingertips until the far wall smoked from the assault.

"Aleksei!"

He jerked and the fireball he threw landed off-target. He spun around and glared. Misha and Sergei stood a few feet from him. When had they arrived?

"What the hell are you doing?" Misha asked.

"What does it look like?" Aleksei snapped.

"It looks like you're ready to fall over," Sergei replied.

"You've been working nonstop for weeks, and now we find you working out like a demon possessed." Misha frowned. "And you look like you've lost weight. If you keep up this pace, you're going to make yourself sick."

"I have a lot to do."

"Then ask for help," Sergei said.

Aleksei glared at Sergei. "Pretty ironic, coming from you. Why would I ask you for help when you'll be hitting the road any day now? That's what you do, Sergei. You run."

"Aleksei—"

Sergei held up his hand. "Don't play peacekeeper, Misha. Just because I haven't stayed here, doesn't mean I ran away. It's not like I can be much help anyway."

Aleksei barked out a harsh laugh. "What a load of bullshit. Why can't you help? Because you don't have any powers? I've got news for you. The only person who cares about that is you. Does it mean you think humans are worthless because they're powerless too? Do you think Misha loves Callie any less because she's human and apparently weak in your eyes?"

Sergei clenched his fists. "Of course not. You're just saying this now because the truth is out, and everyone knows Misha is more powerful than the almighty Aleksei. It's a hard fall from your pedestal, isn't it? Especially now you won't be clan leader."

"Sergei, don't!" Misha growled. "You don't know what's going on."

Aleksei scrubbed his head, then let his hands drop. "Of course not, because he's never here. And that's what you don't understand. Family is there for each other—"

"—I came home when you were in trouble."

"You didn't let me finish. Family is there for both the bad and the good, the big and the small."

"I can't stay here all the time."

"You don't have to be here physically to stay connected to us," Misha said.

Sergei's mouth dropped open. "Shit. I can't believe you're on his side."

"I'm not on anyone's side," Misha barked. "I want us to be in each other's lives."

"Because it's such a barrel of fun?"

"Because I miss you. Because I think we're stronger together than apart. And instead of you two tearing into each other, maybe I should kick both your asses and give you a time out before we continue this conversation!"

Aleksei gaped at Misha. He was the most laid back of the three of them. For him to lose it was monumental. Sergei's surprised expression meant he felt the same. Apparently there was a first time for everything.

Misha crossed his arms. "Now that I have your attention, perhaps we should start this discussion over again. Tell us what's wrong, Aleksei. Does it have to do with a certain portal guard who no longer visits earth?"

Aleksei sidestepped around him. "I need to get cleaned up and ready for work."

"Now who's running?" Sergei called out to him.

Aleksei spun around and faced them. "What do you want me to say? That Naya twists my insides into knots, and I think about her every damn minute of every damn day? She doesn't want to be with me. She doesn't want to be tied down. She wants to be free after the immigration."

Misha's eyes softened, and Aleksei looked away from him. He couldn't handle his pity.

"That doesn't sound like Naya. She is as honorable as you are."

"It doesn't matter. She claims she is going to travel the world with Marrick. And when I confronted him, he told me he's in love with her."

"And?" Misha asked.

Aleksei threw his hands up. "Isn't it enough?"

Misha and Sergei exchanged a glance before Misha continued. "Do you know if she's in love with him? Because that's the only answer that matters."

———————◆◇◆———————

Naya sat down with a sigh at her small table next to the hearth. She was starting to feel tired all the time. Sabrina insisted it was a natural part of pregnancy, but Naya still had work to do. The third group of realm demons would be relocating to earth in the next few weeks.

She sighed again when Marrick opened the door and ushered Sabrina into the room.

"I heard your exasperation through the closed door. I came to check on you, and no complaints from you, lady. Marrick said you look pale." She stared at her for a moment. "You aren't your normal shade of purple. Do you feel okay?"

"I'm fine. Just tired."

"You're working too hard," Marrick said.

She frowned at him. "Females have been having babies since the beginning of time, and they don't sit around doing nothing."

"True, but they do take it easy when their doctor suggests it," Sabrina said. "I wish you would let me take you to earth to do a full workup on you."

"I don't want to see Aleksei."

"Help me understand why."

Naya proceeded to tell Sabina what she had overheard, and how she had told Aleksei she didn't want to be with him.

Sabrina stayed quiet throughout the explanation, until the end. "I understand you are trying to do what you think is best for Aleksei, but did it ever occur to you that he deserves to be part of the decision as well?"

"When he talks about being clan leader, there is light in his eyes. His purpose drives him. I can't take his purpose away."

"So you will keep him away from his child?" Marrick asked.

She rubbed her fingers on her forehead as a headache started to throb. "No. I wouldn't do that to him. I just need more time to figure everything out. I—" She gasped when a hard pinch ran up her back.

Sabrina strode over to her. "What's wrong?"

"It's my back. I've been on my feet too long. I'm sure I'm fine."

Sabrina squatted down and put her hands on Naya's lower back. She rested her hands there for several minutes, until a sharp pinch radiated along her back again.

Sabrina stood up and spoke to Naya. "I think you're having contractions."

Naya rested her hand on her stomach. "I can't be. I'm only six months along."

"I'm taking you to earth, Naya. I can help you and the baby better there. If these are contractions, we can possibly stop them with medicine."

Marrick strode over and scooped Naya up into his arms. "No arguments."

Naya nodded. She wasn't ready to face Aleksei, but she would do anything to protect their baby.

CHAPTER 31

He had been called to meet with his father and the elders. After weeks of his father reading clan bylaws and petitions to change the succession ruling, it was finally time. Aleksei sat on one side of the table facing a line of elders sitting on the other. The us-versus-them seating arrangement did not give him a good feeling about what was about to transpire.

Boris sat at the end of the table with a troubled expression. "We are meeting today to vote on changing the clan leader succession law. I have petitioned the elders to allow me to change the rule concerning awarding clan leadership to the progeny with the strongest powers, and they have agreed."

Aleksei blinked. It was good news...but there had to be something else wrong or Father wouldn't look like he wanted to punch something.

"But?"

"There is a condition," his father said.

Of course there was. "And what is the condition?"

The head elder spoke. "We would like to have an understanding of your future mating plans."

Aleksei frowned. "What exactly do you want to know?"

"We were concerned when you were seen spending time with that portal guard. But we understand any relationship you might have had is no longer an issue."

"And you care because?"

"Because if you become the next clan leader, your children will rule after you. Having a Shamat successor is important to us."

Aleksei gripped his hands into fists. "Any child I had with Naya would be Shamat. I would be their father, and Naya is part Shamat as well."

"We are concerned if the children were to take after the Pavel side. We would have issues with them being clan leader."

"Do you agree with this?" Aleksei asked his father.

"No, and neither does your grandmother, but she has been recused from this conversation since she cannot vote in this matter."

"So you would not consider me if I pursued Naya?"

The elder shrugged. "Since you are no longer associated with her, the answer is not relevant."

Aleksei looked at each elder in turn. "You all agree with this?"

"Not all of us," the last elder at the table said while another agreed with him.

Aleksei looked at them again, one by one. "It is no secret that I have always wanted to rule this clan. I felt it was my duty and my honor to lead after my father steps down. When I found out Misha's powers were stronger than mine, I mourned for the life I had planned since birth.

"But in the past few weeks, I have realized that losing Naya has been much worse. I will not be told by you or anyone else who I can or cannot mate. I am going to fight for Naya. If you feel I cannot lead because of this, then my answer is simple. I won't take over for my father."

The room was silent.

Aleksei glanced in his father's direction, and Boris nodded at him to continue. "Our world is about to change as most of the realm relocates to earth. It might feel overwhelming, but we cannot continue to segregate ourselves. We have done this both between the clans on earth and between earth and the realm. Whether I mate a portal guard or not, we all still have to adapt to our new world. If I don't meet your expectations to lead this clan, then feel free to approach my brothers to see if either of them would like to be clan leader, or you can open it up for election."

Aleksei stood, pushing his chair back with a scrape. "I will leave you to your vote."

He walked toward the door and out into the hall to find his brothers waiting for him.

"How did it go?" Misha asked.

"They were willing to remove the stipulation that the one with stronger powers should rule."

"That's great!" Misha said.

"Until they told me I couldn't mate with Naya and rule."

"What?" Sergei and Misha said simultaneously.

"They don't want a child with Pavel blood ruling the clan."

"And what did you say?" Misha asked.

"I told them in that case I wouldn't rule, and that they could ask one of you, or have an election."

"Holy shit," Sergei blurted. "I'm surprised they didn't all have heart attacks."

"I didn't wait around to find out."

Misha placed his hand on Aleksei's shoulder. "Are you sure about this? You'd be giving up everything you've worked for most of your life."

"Not everything. I'm going to try to win Naya back, if I can convince her to give me a chance now that I won't be ruling. After we finish the realm immigration, I'll do what she wants to do. Go where she wants to go."

"Who are you and what have you done to my brother?" Misha said.

"How many times have you told me to get the stick out of my ass?" Aleksei asked.

"Actually, that was Kyle."

"Well don't tell her I said this, but she was right."

"I heard that," Kyle said as she appeared around the hall corner with a grin.

"How long have you been listening?" Aleksei demanded.

"Long enough to hear you've finally come to your senses, brother."

Before Aleksei could respond to his smart-aleck *sestra*, a guard jogged down the hall toward him.

"What's wrong?" Aleksei asked.

"An unscheduled portal just opened in the compound."

"Are we being attacked?" Misha asked.

"No," the security guard said. "It is Marrick, Naya, and Doctor Miller. Marrick was carrying Naya."

Aleksei tried to absorb the guard's statement. "Where are they now?"

"They went to the infirmary."

Aleksei ran down the hall before the guard could say anything else. Footfalls pounded behind him, but he didn't check to see who followed. He needed to get to Naya to find out if she was okay. He struggled to breathe while he thought of the many things that could have happened to her.

If Marrick carried her here, and Sabrina took her to the infirmary, it must be bad. Every second it took to get to her felt like a new needle jabbing through his skin. He raced across the compound lawn and slammed open the doors of the infirmary, calling out her name, not wanting to waste time by going from room to room.

A door opened and Marrick stepped out into the hall.

"Is she okay?" Aleksei asked.

Marrick held up his hands. "She is with Sabrina."

Aleksei tried to look through the door window, but there was a screen blocking the bed. "What happened? Was she attacked?"

"No. She is ill. Sabrina decided to bring her to earth to check her."

Aleksei tried to walk around Marrick, but he blocked his path.

"What are you doing? Let me pass."

"She doesn't want to see you right now, Aleksei."

The words punctured his chest and he clenched his fists to control his anger. Marrick was larger than he was, but he could still take him.

Hands rested on his shoulders, and Misha spoke from behind him. "Let Sabrina work with her. We don't want to interfere with what's going on. First priority is Naya's health."

His rational brain knew it. But he didn't want to listen to his rational brain, not when his heart was screaming to be heard. He took a step back. "Fine. I'll back off, but I'm not leaving."

Aleksei paced the small waiting room across the hall from Naya. Marrick stood outside her door with his damn arms crossed, and Aleksei glared at him. His brothers and Kyle sat nearby, watching him carefully. "You don't have to stay here with me."

"That's okay. I think we'll stay right here," Misha said.

Sergei nodded.

Footfalls echoed in the corridor and Aleksei rushed over to the door. A nurse was pushing some sort of machine down the hall, and Marrick opened the exam door and let her enter the room.

Aleksei took a step toward the door, and his brothers came up to stand on either side of him. "I'm fine. Tell me what's going on, Marrick."

"I don't know."

He was lying, and Aleksei wanted to punch him in the face.

Why in the hell had she pushed him away? He should have gone to her days ago and insisted she talk to him. If he could convince realm demons to give him a chance, how could he not do the same with the stubborn portal guard who owned his heart?

The nurse rolled the machine next to the bed and Sabrina clicked on some switches. "This is an ultrasound, Naya. We're going to check on the baby and see what's going on."

Naya nodded this time because her throat was locked tight.

Sabrina squirted something cold on her abdomen and then placed a flat instrument against her, slowly pushing it around while paying close attention to a glass on the front of the box. Movement showed on the screen, along with a swooshing sound like water lapping against the beach.

"This is your baby. Right now everything looks normal, except you appear to be having some minor contractions. We're going to give you some medicine to stop them and hook your baby up to a monitor to track vital signs like heartbeat."

"Am I going to lose the baby?"

"I will work very hard to keep your baby in you a while longer. I know it's hard, but we're going to have to wait a little bit to see how you and the baby are doing. I'm going to start an IV now, and get the medicine going to calm down your uterus."

Naya took a deep breath and closed her eyes. For her baby, she would be calm. She couldn't think about anything right now but her baby. Not contractions, or medicine, or the fact that she heard Aleksei call her name earlier. His voice had made her heart slam around in her chest. And that was the opposite of calm.

She would tell him the truth as soon as Sabrina told her the baby was okay.

He had a right to know. And she prayed that when the truth came out he would still be able to lead his clan.

He was born to lead, and the last thing she wanted was to take his destiny away from him.

Chapter 32

Aleksei paced in the hall since the waiting room was now crowded. His babushka and Callie had shown up, and were now also watching him.

The exam room door opened, and Sabrina emerged, closing it behind her.

"How is she?" Aleksei asked as everyone crowded around him.

"She's going to be okay. She isn't injured, but she needed some medical attention."

"Why are you being so damn vague?" Aleksei growled.

"Because I swore an oath as a doctor. It's not my place to give you the specifics about Naya's health."

"Can I see her?"

Sabrina's eyes softened. "In a little bit."

"Sabrina—"

Misha placed his hand on Aleksei's arm. "Don't take your frustration out on Sabrina. She's just doing her job."

He took a deep breath. "I'm sorry." He turned toward his family. "You don't have to stay here anymore."

"We're here to keep watch," Irina announced.

"You heard Sabrina. Naya will be fine," he said, more to convince himself than his family.

"I know Naya is in good hands. I meant you, dear grandson. We're here to watch over you."

Aleksei's glance moved from his grandmother to his brothers, and finally to Kyle. Even she had become the sister he didn't know he wanted.

"Tell us what happened. What we can do to help you win her back," Irina said.

Aleksei looked at Misha who nodded at him to continue. He had already confessed most of this to his brothers. Was he ready to tell Babushka, Callie, and Kyle? "She doesn't want to be with me anymore. Naya said she couldn't be the mate of a clan leader. After years of being a guard in the realm she doesn't want the responsibility."

Kyle frowned. "That doesn't sound like Naya. Didn't you fight for her?"

"Of course I did! I told her I wanted us to be together, that I wouldn't be leading the clan for another century or more, and her feelings might change by that time." He glared at Marrick, who still stood sentry in the hall. "But then she told me she had *an understanding* with *him*."

"No way," Kyle said. "She wouldn't be involved with you and Marrick at the same time."

Aleksei crossed his arms as he confronted Marrick. "What do you have to say about this?"

Marrick stood mute.

"Do you have an understanding with Naya or not?"

Still nothing.

Aleksei's chest tightened as he choked out the words. "You told me you loved her."

Marrick studied him as if trying to read his mind. "I do."

The two simple words stabbed him in the chest and he looked away.

"She is like a sister to me."

Aleksei jerked his head up to look Marrick in the eye.

"I would do anything for her, die for her. We have sworn to protect each other."

"And do you think you need to protect her from me?" Aleksei demanded.

Again with the staring. "No. But that doesn't mean I won't respect her wishes."

"And you believe she doesn't want to see me."

"I think she's confused and scared."

Aleksei struggled for breath. He couldn't bear for his warrior woman to be scared. "Please, Sabrina. I want to talk to her. Can I?"

Sabrina held up her hand in a wait gesture before going back into Naya's room. A few minutes later, she opened the door and beckoned for him to come in.

He took a step into the room, then glanced back to see Marrick and his family crowded in the doorway, shamelessly listening. But the only person he cared about hearing what he had to say was Naya. He walked around the screen and stopped at the end of the bed.

Naya was propped up in the bed, covered with blankets. She had an IV, and monitors were beeping next to her. And she was clearly exhausted. He swallowed down the burn at the back of his throat.

"Naya. Thank the fates you're okay."

"We need to talk, Aleksei."

"Yes."

"I need to tell you someth—"

Was she rejecting him again? Aleksei interrupted her. "Will you let me say something first?"

She nodded.

He cleared his throat. "I was terrified when I found out Marrick had to carry you here. I'm so sorry if I've done something to hurt you. I've been wracking my brain, trying to think of what I said or did to push you away. I know you don't want to be tied down here. That you want to see the world. That you're afraid I'll force you to take on the responsibility of the clan. I won't do that to you. I want to go with you. I want to experience things through your eyes."

Silence.

Aleksei forced himself not to move closer. "Naya?"

"You won't be happy away from your clan, your family."

He whooshed out a breath. From where he stood at the end of the bed, he could see his family in the doorway. Boris had shown up at some point. His father's arm rested on Babushka's shoulders, and Misha and Sergei stood next to them. Even Kyle gave him a thumbs-up.

He turned back to Naya. "I'm surrounded by my family, but I'm not happy now. I miss you. I think about you all the damn time. I miss talking to you and holding you. Hell, I even miss when you argue with me."

"The elders won't let you mate me. And I won't take that away from you. You are meant to lead, Aleksei."

How in the hell did she know what was discussed at the meeting today? "No, Naya. I am meant to be with you. And if it comes down to choosing you or leading the clan, then I choose you. I told the elders as much today."

"You can go back to them and take it back."

"Naya—"

"You still have time."

"Naya! I'm not taking anything back. I love you." Stunned to hear the declaration coming out of his mouth, Aleksei had to grip the bedframe at Naya's feet for balance, and he heard gasps from the doorway. "I. Love. You. Do you...think you could ever love me?"

Aleksei waited. And waited. Painful silent seconds that threatened to flay his insides.

"I love you too, Aleksei."

He wanted to yell and do a dance. Before he could respond, she spoke again.

"But you have a fifty-year plan."

"I do. It only has one item on it. Being with you."

A small sob erupted from Naya's direction.

He wanted to scoop her into his arms and never let her go. "Please, Naya."

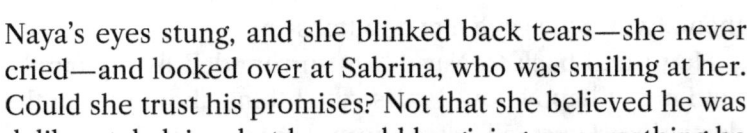

Naya's eyes stung, and she blinked back tears—she never cried—and looked over at Sabrina, who was smiling at her. Could she trust his promises? Not that she believed he was deliberately lying, but he would be giving up something he had worked his whole life to achieve.

"Are you sure, Aleksei? You are giving up your future for me."

He growled. "I am gaining a future with you. You are my heartbeat. Please."

Sabrina held up her hands and gave Naya a penetrating look, as if to say, "what are you waiting for?" Naya nodded and Sabrina beckoned to Aleksei. "Close the door."

Naya heard the door shut, but not before several voices in the hall moaned "no."

She held her breath as Aleksei came around to the end of the bed.

Sabrina backed out of the way as he came closer to Naya, taking her in. She had transitioned to her human form earlier, since it seemed to take less energy to hold it when she wasn't feeling well. He came to her side as she sat up and the blankets fell off her stomach.

He stumbled to a stop.

"Surprise," she said, rubbing her swollen belly.

"Holy Fates...How?" he gasped, looking from her to Sabrina with huge eyes.

"I don't know for sure, but if I had to guess, since neither of you realized she was in her cycle, I think it has to do with Naya traveling back and forth from earth to the realm and the different time fluctuations. We don't have a lot of evidence about how portal-jumping impacts a female's system."

"Are they both okay?" he asked, a tremor in his voice.

Sabrina nodded. "They're both fine. Naya had some early contractions, and we stopped them with some medicine. But she's going to have to take it easy until the baby is born. I want her to stay on bed rest for a while, and then we'll see how she does. Hopefully she won't need to stay in bed for the rest of her pregnancy."

"Thank you," Aleksei said.

Sabrina smiled. "I'll leave you two alone for a couple of minutes, and I'll try to keep your family at bay as long as I can."

Aleksei chuckled. "Good luck with that."

Sabrina left, and he dropped to his knees next to the bed, his hands shaking as he placed them on her bulging belly.

"It's been six weeks since you left me. My brain isn't working right now. How far along are you?"

"About six months."

He dropped his forehead to the bed.

She reached up and threaded her fingers through his dark hair. Was this too much for him? A male who needed order and consistency in his life? He had just thrown away his chance to lead for her—before he found out he was going to be a father.

"Aleksei?"

He looked up at her, and she gasped. His eyes were wet, and a giant smile covered his face.

"I love you so much. And I love this baby."

She studied his face. "You're not upset?"

"Not for the reason you think. This baby is a blessing. I'm upset that you didn't tell me when you found out."

"I didn't want you to lose your chance to lead."

"How do you even know that? I only spoke to the elders today."

"The last time I was on earth, I heard them talking about not letting you lead if you mated with me. That your children would have Pavel in them, and they didn't want Pavel blood in their clan leader."

His eyes narrowed on her. "Is that why you left?"

"Yes."

"So the story you gave me about not wanting to be with me and wanting to travel around was an excuse."

She nodded slowly, since his eyes had just turned black, which meant his demon was close to the surface.

"Female, I would spank you right now if I could. Don't you ever do that again. Going forward, we will make decisions together."

She opened her mouth and he glared at her. She wasn't going to argue with him. "Okay. Do you think we should save Sabrina and let your family in?"

He smiled his brilliant smile at her. "Soon. I want to spend a couple more moments with you and our baby."

He stood and kissed her stomach lightly before leaning up to kiss her lips. He rested his forehead against her and took a deep breath. "Are you ready for this?"

"Yes."

He pushed back the screen and opened the door. Seconds later, the small room was mobbed with Kyle, Irina, Boris, Sergei, Callie, Misha...and Marrick, who stayed by the door.

Kyle gasped. "Oh, my God, a secret demon baby. I'm living in a romance novel!"

Irina squealed as well. "More grandbabies. First the twins, and now this." She smacked Aleksei in the shoulder. "How could you not have told us?"

"I didn't know."

The excited chatter stopped, and they all gaped at him until Misha and Boris burst out laughing and Sergei covered his mouth with his hand.

"Don't say a word," Aleksei said in a threatening tone, which just made the males laugh harder.

"I didn't think I had to have the safe sex talk with you, Aleksei," Boris said as he wiped his eyes.

"Leave Naya and Aleksei alone," Callie admonished the rest of them.

Aleksei went to Marrick and grabbed the male to pull him close in a one-armed hug. "Thank you for watching over her."

Marrick slapped his back before stepping back. "Of course."

Naya shook her head. "All right, you two. I can take care of myself."

Aleksei and Marrick grinned at each other before Aleksei spoke. "Of course you can, my dear. But the point is, you don't have to all the time. We'll take care of each other."

She nodded. "Good answer."

"I'm so proud of you, son," Boris said. "Someday you and Naya will be running the clan."

"What are you talking about? You heard what I said to the elders today."

"I did. But you didn't hear what the elders said after you left the room. They agreed that you should lead, Aleksei. You didn't back down from their threats, and when it came down to it, they chose someone who is willing to stand up for what or who they believe in."

Aleksei blinked for a moment and then looked over at her. "I'll have to talk to Naya about what she wants to do as well. This isn't just my choice."

Naya blinked but tears escaped...apparently she did cry...and reached for his hand.

"All right, wonderful family of mine," Aleksei announced. "It's time to let Naya rest."

Everyone filed out of the room except Aleksei, who hadn't let go of her hand.

"I promise to stay in bed tonight. Why don't you go get some sleep?"

He shook his head. "I'm not going anywhere." He crawled into bed with her, making sure he didn't disturb her IV, and held her. "You're not getting rid of me any time soon."

He snuggled close to her.

"We've got a lot to think about, to plan," Naya said.

"The only change in my fifty-year plan is that I will be spending lots of time with you *and* our child. The rest we'll figure out as it comes."

He kissed her hair, and she rested her head against his chest, breathing him in and letting him settle in her soul before his heartbeat lulled her to sleep.

CHAPTER 33

Three Weeks Later

"Aleksei Chesnokov! I am perfectly capable of walking!"

Aleksei grinned down at Naya while he carried her across the lawn to the large table set up for the celebratory dinner. They were celebrating another successful immigration. This time, a group of fifty had arrived and were now being acclimated to earth.

"I know, Naya. But you've been in bed for a while now, and Sabrina only today released you from bed rest. She said for you to take it easy. I am merely following doctor's orders."

She rolled her eyes at him and he laughed.

"You're spending too much time with Kyle," he said, and he set her down in a chair and kissed the top of her head before greeting the rest of the guests who were just now showing up for the dinner.

Irina sat down next to her and grasped her hand. "I want to thank you."

"For what?"

"Bringing out the best in my grandson. I always knew he would grow into his leadership role, but I worried that he would never let go of his rigid guidelines. You have shown him life is also about spontaneity and love."

Naya blinked back tears. For someone who hadn't cried once in her whole life, she had certainly made up for it in the past few days. "He has taught me as well."

"I knew you would be good together. First we had to straighten out Misha, and then I had to prod Aleksei a little as well."

"Did you conduct some sort of intervention I'm unaware of?"

"No. I simply planted the seeds with Aleksei. Told him about all the single males flocking around you at breakfast. That sort of thing. I'm glad he finally opened his eyes and saw you."

"Would it surprise you if I said I seduced him?"

Irina burst out laughing. "Even better! I knew I liked you from the moment we met."

"What are you two laughing about?" Aleksei asked from behind them.

"Nothing, my dear. Can't a grandmother enjoy her new granddaughter?"

Naya sucked in a breath at her words, and Irina patted her hand. "You are my granddaughter now, and there will be no fighting me on this."

Naya nodded.

Aleksei sat down on the other side of Naya and wrapped his arm around her shoulders. "She's right. There is no fighting Babushka."

Boris called out to the group for everyone to take their seats. He held up his glass and spoke to the long table of guests. "Thank you for all your hard work in making the latest immigration a success."

Aleksei handed Naya her water glass, and she mimicked everyone else when they held up their glasses, clinked them together, and then took a sip.

Boris encouraged everyone to start eating, but first Naya wanted to look around at all the people. Kyle sat with the rest of the BSR team, and was obviously teasing her mate,

Dalton. Across from them sat Callie and Misha with the twins. Even Sergei was attending the dinner.

Callie was whispering in Misha's ear as he leaned forward to fill his plate. Suddenly the serving spoon fell out of his hand, clattering against his plate. Everyone turned toward them.

"Is everything okay, Mikhail?" Irina asked.

"Yes. Um... I'm not really very hungry."

Silence.

Misha's face turned bright red.

"If you keep losing your appetite, you might want to have the doctor check you over, brother," Aleksei said with a ridiculous grin on his face.

"I think we're going to c-call it a n-night," Misha stuttered.

"Of course, dear. It's been a long day for everyone," Irina said.

Misha stood and pulled out Callie's chair.

"Aren't you going to stay for dessert?" Luke asked.

"I've got some dessert at the house," Callie said at the same moment Kyle choked on a sip of water.

"You boys be good for Miss Irina tonight," Callie said.

"Yes, Momma," they chorused.

Before Callie could say any more goodbyes, Misha dragged her along the back of the house toward the sidewalk.

Naya and Irina chuckled.

"What did I miss?" Aleksei asked.

Irina winked at him. "Callie asked me to watch the boys tonight so they can have some alone time. With the boys, and the hectic schedule we've been keeping, they haven't had a chance to..."

"...knock boots," Naya finished the sentence.

Irina's tinkling laugh turned into a guffaw. "Precisely."

"You really have been spending too much time with Kyle," Aleksei said.

Naya eyed him, brows raised. "There's nothing wrong with Kyle. She's a strong woman, and she will be a part of our child's life."

"That's what I'm afraid of," Aleksei said as he served himself some food.

"Our baby will be surrounded by love, and she will be all the better for it."

The serving spoon in Aleksei's hand clattered to the tray and the table stopped talking and turned to look. Again.

"The baby is a she?" He turned to her and grabbed her hands.

"Yes. We're having a girl. I was going to tell you later." Naya looked around at all the gaping faces. "In private," she whispered.

The group started cheering and clapping. Aleksei stood and scooped Naya up into his arms and carried her away.

"Are you happy?" she asked.

His eyes shone with unshed tears. "The idea of having a daughter who takes after her strong, intelligent, beautiful mother is more than I could ever have hoped for."

"I'm glad. You do know you're going to have to stop carrying me around everywhere, right?"

"Yes... Maybe... Eventually."

"What am I going to do with you, Aleksei?"

He leaned down for a kiss and then pulled back the space of a breath.

"Just love me," he whispered.

"Sounds like a wonderful plan," she said, right before his lips found hers again.

THANKS!

Thank you for taking the time to read *Demons Are A Girl's Best Friend*. Sergei's story, *Demons Are Forever*, is next. You caught a glimpse of him in Aleksei's story...

I hope you enjoyed Aleksei's happy ending and the second book in the Realm Series. Please consider telling your friends about it or posting a short review. Word of mouth is an author's best friend, and much appreciated. Thank you!
– AE

If you would like to know when my next books will be released, please check out my website aejonesauthor.com

Please turn the page to find a list of my other books.

Other Books By AE

Mind Sweeper Series
Mind Sweeper
The Fledgling
Shifter Wars
The Pursuit
Sentinel Lost

The Realm Series (Mind Sweeper Spin Off)
Demons Will Be Demons
Demons Are A Girl's Best Friend
Demons Are Forever
Demons In The Rough
Demons Just Want To Have Fun

The Pack Series (Mind Sweeper Spin Off)
Shifter and the Succubus

Paranormal Wedding Planner Series
In Sickness and In Elf
From This Fae Forward
To Have and To Howl
For Better or For Wolf
For Witch or For Poorer
Till Demon Do Us Part

The Sentries Series
Dragon Kissed
Dragon Charmed

ACKNOWLEDGMENTS

Special thanks to my normal cast of characters, including Faith, my editor, and Amy my awesome proofreader.

A shout out to my beta readers, Sandy and Becky. And many thanks to Becky Lower for pointing out a few things that could use tightening up in the story.

As always, to my family who are some of my biggest fans. Thanks for your unwavering support.

And to you, my readers, who inspire me to write and to turn a once egotistical demon, into one we could fall in love with.

ABOUT THE AUTHOR

Growing up a TV junkie, AE Jones oftentimes rewrote endings of episodes in her head when she didn't like the outcome. She immersed herself in sci-fi and soap operas. But when *Buffy* hit the little screen, she knew her true love was paranormal. Now she spends her nights weaving stories about all variations of supernatural—their angst and their humor. After all, life is about both...whether you sport fangs or not.

AE won the prestigious Golden Heart® Award for her paranormal manuscript, Mind Sweeper, which also was a RITA® finalist for both First Book and Paranormal Romance. AE is also a recipient of the Booksellers' Best Award and is a National Readers' Choice Award Finalist, Holt Award of Merit Finalist and a Daphne du Maurier Finalist.

AE lives in Ohio surrounded by her eclectic family and friends who in no way resemble any characters in her books. *Honest.* Now her two cats are another story altogether.

Learn more about AE and her books on her website aej onesauthor.com